DEMELZA

DEMELZA

VOLUME II

A Novel of Cornwall
1788 - 1790

Winston Graham

G.K.HALL&CO.

Boston, Massachusetts

1979

Library of Congress Cataloging in Publication Data

Graham, Winston.
   Demelza : a novel of Cornwall, 1788-1790.

   Large print ed.
   1.   Large type books.   I.   Title.
[PZ3.G76246De 1979]   [PR6013.R24]   823'.9'12   78-26791
ISBN 0-8161-6677-3

Published in Large Print by arrangement with Doubleday & Company, Inc.

Set in Photon 18 pt Crown

DEMELZA

BOOK THREE

CHAPTER I

"Read me the story of the Lost Miner, Aunt Verity," Geoffrey Charles said.

"I have read it you once already."

"Well, again, please. Just like you read it last time."

Verity picked up the book and absently ruffled Geoffrey Charles's curly head. Then a pang went through her that at this time to-morrow she would not be there to read to him.

The windows of the big parlour were open, and the July sun lay across the room. Elizabeth sat embroidering a waistcoat, with dusty sun bars touching colour in her beige silk frock. Aunt Agatha, having no truck with fresh air, crouched before the small fire she insisted on their keeping and drowsed like a tired old cat, the Bible, this being Sunday, open loosely in her lap. She did not move at all, but every now and then her eyes would open sharply as if she had heard a mouse in the wainscot. Geoffrey Charles, in a velvet suit and long velvet trousers, was a weight on Verity's knee where she sat by the window in the half shadow of a lace curtain. Francis was somewhere about the farm. In the two topped beech trees across the lawn pigeons were cooing.

Verity finished the story and slid Geoffrey Charles gently to the floor.

''There is mining in his blood, Elizabeth,'' she said. ''No other story will suit.''

Elizabeth smiled without looking up.

''When he grows up conditions may have changed.'' Verity rose. ''I do not think I will go to Evensong. I have a headache.''

''It will be with sitting in the sun. You sit too much in the sun, Verity.''

''I must go now and see about the wine. You can never trust Mary to look at it, for she falls into a daydream when she should not.''

''I'll come with you,'' said Geoffrey Charles. ''Let me help you, eh?''

While she was busy in the kitchen Francis came in. This summer he had been trying to help about the farm. The work somehow did not suit him; it sat bleakly on his nature. Geoffrey Charles ran towards him but, seeing the expression on his father's face, changed his mind and ran back to Verity.

Francis said: "Tabb is the only man left with any farming in him. Ellery is worse than useless. He was told to rebuild the hedge in the sheep field, and it has broke in a week. It has taken us best part of an hour to get the flock back. I'll turn the fellow off."

"Ellery has been a miner since he was nine."

"That's the whole trouble," Francis said wryly. He looked at his hands, which were caked with dirt. "We do our best for these local people, but how can you expect miners to become hedgers and ditchers overnight?"

"Are the oats undamaged?"

"Yes, thanks be. By a mercy the first sheep turned down the lane instead of up."

The oats were to be cut next week. She

would not be here for it. She could hardly believe that.

"I shall not come to church this evening, Francis. I have a headache. I think it's the warm weather."

"I'm much of a mind to stay away myself," he said.

"Oh, you can't do that." She tried to hide her alarm. "They're expecting you."

"Elizabeth can go by herself. She will stand for the family well enough."

Verity bent over the boiling wine and skimmed it. "Mr. Odgers would be heartbroken. He was telling me only last week that he always chooses the shortest psalms and preaches a special sermon for Evensong to please you."

Francis went out without replying, and Verity found that her hands were trembling. Geoffrey Charles's chatter, which had broken out again when his father went, was a tinkling noise that came to her from a distance. She had chosen Sunday at four as the only time of the week when she could be sure of Francis's being out. His movements these last months had been unpredictable; to this conventional habit he had been faithful. . . .

"Auntie Verity!" cried the boy. "Auntie Verity! Why don't you?"

"I can't listen to you now, sweetheart," she said abruptly. "Please leave me alone." She tried to take hold of herself, went into the next kitchen, where Mary Bartle was sitting, and spoke to her for a few minutes.

"Auntie Verity. Auntie Verity. Why aren't any of you going to church this afternoon?"

"I am not. Your father and mother will be going."

"But Father just said he was not."

"Never mind. You stay and help Mary with the wine. Be careful you don't get in her way."

"But if——"

She turned quickly from the kitchen and, instead of walking through the house, went quickly across the courtyard with its disused fountain and came in at the big hall. She ran up the stairs. It might be the last time she would see Geoffrey Charles, but there was no chance of saying good-bye.

In her bedroom she went quickly to the window. From this corner of it, by pressing her face against the glass, she could just see the drive by which Francis and Elizabeth would walk to church — if they were going.

Very faintly in the distance the bells had begun to ring. Number three was slightly cracked and Francis always said it set his teeth on edge. Francis would take ten minutes or a quarter of an hour to put on clean linen. She expected that at this moment he and Elizabeth were debating whether he should go or not. Elizabeth would want him to go. Elizabeth must make him go.

She sat there stilly on the window seat, a curious chill creeping into her body from the touch of the glass. She couldn't for a second take her eyes from that corner of the drive.

She knew exactly how the bell ringers would look, sweating there in the enclosed space of the tower. She knew how each one of the choir would look, fumbling in the pews for their psalters, exchanging whispers, talking more openly when she did not come. Mr. Odgers would be bustling about in his surplice, poor, thin, harassed little fellow. They would all miss her, not merely to-night but in the future. And surely all the people whom she visited, the sick and the crippled, and the women struggling, overburdened with their families. . . .

She felt the same about her own family. Had times been good she would have left with a much freer heart. Elizabeth was not strong, and it would mean another woman to help Mrs. Tabb. More expense when every shilling counted. And no one could do just what she had done, holding all the strings of the house economically together, keeping a tight but friendly hold.

Well, what other way was open? She couldn't expect Andrew to wait longer. She had not seen him in the three months since the ball, all word having gone through Demelza. She had already put off her flight once because of Geoffrey Charles's illness. It was almost as bad now, but leave she must or stay for ever.

Her heart gave a leap. Elizabeth was

walking down the drive, tall and slender and so graceful in her silk frock and straw hat and cream parasol. Surely she could not be going alone. . . .

Francis came into view. . . .

She got up from the window. Her cheek had stuck to the glass and it tingled sharply with returning blood. She looked unsteadily round the room. She knelt and from under the bed drew out her bag. Geoffrey Charles would still be running about, but she knew how to avoid him.

With the bag she came to the door, stared back round the room. The sun was shining aslant the tall old window. She slipped quickly out and leaned back against the door trying to get her breath. Then she set off towards the back stairs.

Having given way to Elizabeth and made the effort to go to church, Francis had felt a slow change of mood. This country farmer-squire life he led left him bored and frustrated almost to death. He longed for the days he had lost. But now and then, since all things are relative, his boredom waned and he forgot his frustration. It was the more strange to-day since he had been so angry over the sheep; but the afternoon was so perfect that it left no room in a man's soul for discontent. Walking here with the sun-warmed air on his face he had come up against the fact that it was good just to be alive.

There was perhaps a certain pleasure in finding most of the congregation waiting outside for them, ready to bob or touch their hats as they came by. After grubbing about the farm all week one was curiously grateful for this buttress to one's self-esteem.

Even the informal sight of Jud Paynter sitting on one of the distant gravestones drinking a mug of ale was not to be cavilled at.

The church was warm but did not smell so strongly as usual of mildew and worm and stale breath. The thin little curate bobbing about like an earwig was not an active irritation; and Joe Permewan, rasping away at the bass viol as if it were a tree trunk, was worth liking as well as laughing at. Joe, they all knew, was no angel and got drunk Saturday nights, but he always sawed his way back to salvation on a Sunday morning.

They had said the psalms and read the lessons and echoed the prayers, and Francis had been gently dozing off to sleep when the sudden bang of the church door roused him. A new worshipper had come in.

Jud had been to France for a couple of nights and had been merrying himself on the share-out. Sobriety never turned him to his Maker, but as always when the drink was in him he felt the urge to reform. And to reform not only himself but all men. He felt the fraternal pull. This afternoon he had wandered from the kiddleys and was in fresh fields.

As Mr. Odgers gave out the psalm he came slowly down the aisle, fingering his cap and blinking in the semi-dark. He took a seat and dropped his cap, then he bent to pick it up and knocked over the stick of old Mrs. Carkeek sitting next to him. After the clatter had died he pulled out a large red rag and began to mop his fringe.

"Some hot," he said to Mrs. Carkeek,

thinking to be polite.

She took no notice but stood up and began to sing.

Everyone in fact was singing, and the people in the gallery by the chancel steps were making the most noise of all and playing instruments just like a party. Jud sat where he was, mopping himself and staring round the church. All this was very new to him. He looked on it in a detached and wavering light.

Presently the psalm was done and everybody sat down. Jud was still staring at the choir.

"What're all they women doin' up there?" he muttered, leaning over and breathing liquorously on Mrs. Carkeek.

"Sh-sh. Tis the choir," she whispered back.

"What, they, the choir? Be they nearer Heaven than we folk?"

Jud brooded a minute. He was feeling kindly but not as kindly as all that. "Mary Ann Tregaskis. What she done to be nearer Heaven than we?"

"Ssh! Ssh!" said several people around him.

He had not noticed that Mr. Odgers had come to be standing in the pulpit.

Jud blew his nose and put the rag away in his pocket. He turned his attention to Mrs. Carkeek, who was sitting primly fingering her cotton gloves.

"Ow's your old cow?" he whispered. "Calved yet, have she?"

Mrs. Carkeek seemed to find a flaw in one of the gloves and gave it all her attention.

"Reckon 'er's going to be one of the awkward ones. Reckon ye did no good by yerself, buyin' of 'er from old Uncle Ben. Slippery ole twitch, he be, and in the choir at that. . . ."

Suddenly a voice spoke loudly, as it were just above his head. It quite startled him, seeing that everyone else seemed afraid of speaking a word.

"My text is from Proverbs Twenty-three, verse Thirty-one. 'Look not thou upon the wine when it is red. At the last it stingeth like an adder and biteth like a serpent.' "

Jud raised his head and saw Mr. Odgers in a sort of wooden box with a sheaf of papers in his hands and an old pair of spectacles on his nose.

"My friends," said Mr. Odgers, looking round, "I have chosen the text for this week after due thought and anxious prayer. My reason for so doing is that on Thursday next we celebrate Sawle Feast. As you all know, this holiday has long been the occasion not merely for harmless healthy jollification but for excessive indulgence in drink. . . ."

"Earear," said Jud, not quite to himself.

Mr. Odgers broke off and looked down severely at the bald old man sitting just below him. After staring for a moment and hearing nothing more he went on:

"For excessive indulgence in drink. It is my plea this evening to the members of the congregation that on Thursday next they should set a shining example in the parish. We have to remember, dear friends, that this feast day is no time for drunkenness and debauchery; for it was instituted to commemorate the landing of our patron saint, St. Sawle, from Ireland, who came to convert the heathens of west

Cornwall. It was in the fourth century that he floated over from Ireland on a millstone and——"

"On a what?" Jud asked.

"On a millstone," Mr. Odgers said, forgetting himself. "It is a historical fact that he landed——"

"Well, I only axed!" whispered Jud in irritation to the man behind, who had tapped him on the shoulder.

"*Sanctus Sawlus,*" said Mr. Odgers, "that is the motto of our church, and it should be a motto and a precept for our daily lives. One which we bear with us as St. Sawle brought it to our shores——"

"On a millstone," muttered Jud to Mrs. Carkeek. "Who ever 'eard of a man floating on a millstone. Giss along! Tedn sense, tedn reasonable, tedn right, tedn proper, tedn true!"

"You will see that we have with us to-day," said Mr. Odgers, rashly accepting the challenge, "one who habitually looks upon the wine when it is red. So the Devil enters into him and leads him into a house of God to flaunt his wickedness in our faces——"

" 'Ere," said Jud unsteadily. "I aren't no different not from them up there. What you got in the choir, eh? Naught but drunkers and whores' birds! Look at old Uncle Ben Tregeagle with 'is ringlets, settin' up there all righteous. And he'd do down a poor old widow woman by sellin' 'er a cow what he know is going to misfire."

The man behind grasped his arm. "Here, you come on out."

Jud thrust him back in his seat with the flat of his hand.

"I aren't doing no harm! Tes that little owl up there as be doing the harm. 'Im an' his whores' birds. Tellin' a wicked ole yarn about a man *floating* on a millstone. . . ."

"Come along, Paynter," said Francis, who had been urged by Elizabeth. "Air your grievances outside. If you come disturbing us in church you are likely to end up in gaol."

Jud's bloodshort eyes travelled over Francis. Injured, he said: "What for d'ye turn me out, eh? I'm a fisherman now, not nobody's servant, an' I know millstones no

531

more float than fly.''

Francis took his arm. "Come along, man.''

Jud detached his arm. "I'll go,'' he said with dignity. He added loudly: "Tes a poor murky way ye take to repentance by followin' the likes of he. Ye'll go to the furnace, sure as me name's Jud Paynter. The flesh'll sweal off of yer bones. A fine lot of dripping ye'll make. Especially old Mrs. Grubb there, 'oo's taken' up two seats wi' her fat! And Char Nanfan in the choir expectin' of 'er third!''

Two large men began to lead him up the aisle.

" 'Ullo, Mrs. Metz, buried any more husbands, 'ave ee? Why and there's Johnnie Kimber as stole a pig. And little Betty Coad. Well, well. Not wed yet, Betty? Tes 'igh time . . .''

They got him to the door. Then he shook himself free and sent out a last blast.

"Twon't always be the same as this, friends. There's doings in France, friends. There's riots and bloody murder! They've broke open the prison an' the Governor's 'ead they've stuck on a pole! There'll be bonfires for some folk here afore ever they die! I tell ee——"

The door slammed behind him and only distant shouting could be heard as he was led to the lych gate.

People slowly began to settle down again. Francis, half annoyed, half amused, picked up a couple of prayer books and returned to his pew.

"Well," said Mr. Odgers, mopping his brow, "as I was saying, quite apart from the — er — legend or — er — miracle of St. Sawle . . ."

CHAPTER II

They walked home with Mr. and Mrs. Odgers. Francis admitted the arguments of his womenfolk that, with ten children to feed, this was probably the only square meal the Odgers got in a week (and this not so immensely square as it had once been); but it did not make them any better company. He would not have minded so much if they had been less agreeable. Sometimes he twisted his own opinions just to take a contrary view and found amusement in watching Odgers's acrobatics in following. One thing the Odgers were obstinately determined not to do and that was fall out with the Poldarks.

They walked home in twos, the ladies on ahead, the gentlemen pacing behind. Oh, lord, thought Francis, if only the man could play hazard and had money to lose.

"That fellow Paynter is going to the dogs," he said. "I wonder why my cousin got rid of him? He stood enough ill behaviour from him in the past."

"It was some scandal he spoke, so I heard. The man is a thorough-going scoundrel, sir. He deserves to be put in the stocks. I do not think the congregation ever settled down proper after he left."

Francis suppressed a smile. "I wonder what he had to say of France. Was he making it all up, I wonder?"

"There has been some story about, Mr. Poldark. My wife in the course of her parish duties had occasion to visit Mrs. Janet Trencrom — you know, the niece-by-marriage of *the* Mr. Trencrom. Mrs. Trencrom said—— Now what were her words? Maria! What was it Mrs. Trencrom told you?"

"Oh, well, Mrs. Trencrom said they were full of it in Cherbourg, but of course it will have been magnified. She said that French prison — what is it called? — was overthrown by rioters about Tuesday or Wednesday last and the Governor and many of his men slaughtered."

"I query the truth of it," Francis said, after a moment.

"I trust there is *no* truth in it," Mr. Odgers said vehemently. "Mob law is always to be deplored. That man, Paynter, for instance, is a dangerous type. He would have the houses about our ears if we gave him half a chance."

Francis said: "When there are riots in this country they are not led or incited by tipsy old men. There, Odgers, look at that field of oats. If the weather holds we shall begin to cut to-morrow."

At Trenwith Francis led the little curate out into the garden while the ladies tidied themselves. When they went into the winter parlour for supper and Mrs. Odgers's small, anxious grey eyes were glistening at the sight of all the food, Francis said:

"Where's Verity?"

"I went to her bedroom as soon as I came back, but she was not there," Elizabeth said.

Francis put his mouth against Aunt

Agatha's long pointed ear.

"Have you seen Verity?"

"What? Eh?" Aunt Agatha rested on her sticks. "Verity? Out, I believe."

"Out? Why should she go out at this time?"

"Leastwise, I fancy she be. She came and kissed me an hour gone and she had on her cloak and things. I didn't gather what she said; folk mumble so. If they was learned to talk out like they was learned in my young days there'd be less trouble in the world. No mines working. I tell ye, Francis, tis a poor world for the old and aged. There's some that would go to the wall. Nay, Odgers, I tell you myself, there's little comfort in——"

"Did she say where she was going?"

"What? Verity? I tell you I could catch nothin' she said. But she left some sort of letter for you both."

"A letter?" said Elizabeth, jumping at the truth far before Francis. "Where is it?"

"Well, aren't you goin' to ask to see it? Damme, no curiosity these days. I wonder what I did with it. It was just here in my shawl." She hobbled to the table and sat down, her wrinkled old hands fumbling in the laces and folds of her clothes. Mr. Odgers waited impatiently until he too could sit down and begin on the cold fowl and the gooseberry pies.

A couple of lice were all she disturbed at first, but presently one claw came trembling out with a sealed paper between finger and thumb.

"I thought it smelt somewhat of an insult puttin' wax on a letter I was to carry," said the old lady. "Eh? What d'you say? As if I cared for Miss Verity's secrets. . . . I bring to mind well the day she was born. The winter o' fifty-nine. Twas just after the rejoicings on the takin' of Quebec, and me and your father had rid over to a bearbaiting at St. Ann's. We'd scarce got home and inside the house when——"

"Read this," said Francis, thrusting the open letter towards Elizabeth. His small features were pinched with a sudden uncontrollable anger.

Her eyes glanced swiftly over it.

I have known and loved you all my life, dear Francis [*it ran*], and you Elizabeth more than seven years, so I pray you will both understand the grief and loss I feel that this should be our Parting. For three months and more I have been torn two ways by loyalties and effections which lived and grew in me with equal Strength, and which in happier circumstances could have existed without conflict. That of the two I have chosen to tear up the deeper rooted and follow after a Life and destiny of my own with a man whom you distrust may seem to you the height of folly, but I pray you will not look on it as a desertion. I am to live in Falmouth now. Oh, my dears, I should have been so happy if only distence were to separate us . . .

"Francis!" Elizabeth said. "Where are you going?"

"To see how she went — if there is time to bring her back!" He left the room with a sudden swing.

"What's to do?" asked Agatha. "What's

got him? What does the note say?"

"Forgive me." Elizabeth turned to the gaping Odgers. "There is — I am afraid there has been some misunderstanding. Do please sit down and have your supper. Don't wait for us. I am afraid we shall be a little time." She followed Francis.

The four remaining house servants were in the big kitchen. The Tabbs, just back from church, were telling the Bartles about Jud Paynter. The laughter stopped suddenly when they saw Francis.

"At what time did Miss Verity leave this house?"

"Oh, an hour and a half gone, sur," said Bartle, glancing curiously at his master's face. "Just after you'd gone church, sur."

"What horse did she take?"

"Her own, sur. Ellery went with her."

"Ellery. . . . Was she carrying anything?"

"I dunno, sur. He's back in the stables now, just giving the 'orses their fodder."

"Back . . .?" Francis checked himself, and went swiftly out to the stables. The horses were all there. "Ellery!" he shouted. The man's startled face appeared round the door.

"Sur?"

"I understand you have been riding with Miss Verity. Is she back with you?"

"No, sur. She changed 'orses at Bargus Cross. A gentleman was waiting for her there with a spare 'orse, and she changed over to 'is and sent me back."

"What sort of gentleman?"

"Seafaring I should guess, sur. Leastwise, by his clothes . . ."

An hour and a half. They would already be beyond Truro. And they could take two or three different routes. So she had come to this. She had made up her mind to mate herself with this wife-kicking drunkard, and nothing should stop her. Blamey had the Devil's power over her. No matter what his record or his ways, he had but to whistle and she would run.

When Francis got back to the kitchen Elizabeth was there.

"No, mistress," Mary Bartle was saying. "I don't know nothing about that, mistress."

"Ellery is back without her," Francis said. "Now, Tabb; and you, Bartle; and you women; I want to hear the truth. Has Miss Verity been receiving letters through your hands?"

"No, sur. Oh, no, sur," they chorused.

"Come, let's talk it over quietly," Elizabeth suggested. "There is little we can do at present."

But Francis was bitterly careless of appearances. He knew it must all come out in a day or two. He would be the butt of the district: the man who tried to stop his sister's courting, and she calmly eloping one afternoon while he was at church.

"There must have been some contact unknown to us," he said sharply to Elizabeth. "Have any of you seen a seafaring man hanging about the grounds?"

No, they had seen nothing.

"She has been out and about visiting poor people in Sawle and Grambler, you know," Elizabeth said.

"Has anyone been calling here unknown to us?" Francis demanded. "Someone who saw Miss Verity and might have carried a message?"

No, they had seen no one.

"Mistress Poldark from Nampara has been over often enough," said Mary Bartle. "By the kitchen way——"

Mrs. Tabb trod on her toe, but it was too late. Francis stared at Mary Bartle for a moment or two, then went out, slamming the door behind him.

Elizabeth found him in the large parlour standing, hands behind back, at the window, looking over the garden.

She closed the door to let him know she was there, but he did not speak.

"We must accept the fact of her going, Francis," she said. "It is her choice. She is grown-up and a free agent. In the last resort we could never have stopped her if she had chosen to go. I could only have wished she had done it openly if she was to do it at all."

"Damn Ross!" Francis said between his teeth. "This is his doing, his and that impudent brat he married. Don't you see . . . he — he has stored this up all these years. Five years ago, knowing we disapproved, he gave them leave to meet at his house. He encouraged Verity in the teeth of all we said. He has never got over his defeat. He never liked to be the loser in anything. I wondered how Verity met this fellow again; no doubt it was at Ross's contrivance. And for these last months after my quarrel with Blamey, knowing I had broken the link again, he has been acting as agent for Blamey, keeping the skunk's interests warm and using Demelza as a postman and go-between!''

"I think you're a little hasty," Elizabeth said. "So far we don't even know that Demelza is concerned in it, let alone Ross."

"Of course," he said passionately, still not turning from the window, "you will always stand up for Ross in all things. You never imagine that Ross could do anything to our disadvantage."

"I am not standing up for anyone," Elizabeth said, a spark of anger in her voice. "But it is the merest justice not to condemn people unheard."

"The facts shout aloud for anyone with half an ear. There's no other way Blamey could have arranged her flight. She has had no post. I've seen to that. Demelza alone could not have done it, for she never knew Blamey in the old days. Ross has been riding about all over the countryside on his damned copper concerns. What more easy than to call in at Falmouth from time to time and bear a message both ways.''

''Well, there's nothing we can do about it now. She is gone. I don't know what we shall do without her. The busiest season of the year; and Geoffrey Charles will miss her terribly.''

''We'll get along. Be sure of that.''

''We should go back to the Odgers,'' Elizabeth said. ''They'll think us very rude. There's nothing to do to-night, Francis.''

''I want no supper just yet. They'll not mind my absence so long as they're fed themselves.''

''What must I tell them?''

''The truth. It will be all over the district in a day or two anyway. Ross should be pleased.''

There was a tap on the door before Elizabeth could open it.

"If you please, sir," said Mary Bartle, "Mr. Warleggan has called."

"Who?" said Francis. "Devil take it! I wonder if he has some news."

George came in, well groomed, polite, heavy in the shoulders and formidable. A rare visitor these days.

"Ah, well, I'm glad to find you have finished supper. Elizabeth, that simple dress suits you to——"

"Good God, we haven't yet begun it!" Francis said. "Have you brought news of Verity?"

"Is she away?"

"Two hours since. She has gone to that skunk Blamey!"

George glanced quickly from one to the other, sizing up their moods, not pleased by his brusque greeting. "I'm sorry. Is there anything I can do?"

"No, it's hopeless," Elizabeth said. "I have told Francis we must swallow it. He has been quite raving since. We have the Odgers here and they'll think we have all gone crazy. Forgive me, George, I must go and see if they have begun supper."

She swept past George, whose admiring

glance flickered after her. Then he said: "You should know, Francis, that women can't be reasoned with. They are a headstrong sex. Let her have her bit, dear boy. If she falls at a fence it will be none of your doing."

Francis pulled at the bell. "I can't face those two agreeable sheep for supper. Your arrival on a Sunday evening was so unexpected that for a moment I hoped . . . How I hate the thought of that fellow getting his way with her after all!"

"I have spent the day at the Teagues' and was feeling monstrous tired of the old lady's chatter, so I thought of an agreeable duty to perform at Trenwith. Poor Patience. There she sits on the hook, waiting for me to bite; a nice enough girl in an oncoming sort of way, but no true breeding about her. I'll swear her legs are on the short side. The woman I marry must not only have the right blood but show it."

"Well, you have come to a household that'll offer you no graces to-night, George. Oh, Mrs. Tabb, serve supper in here. Bring half of one of the boiled fowls

547

if the Odgers have not yet picked 'em clean, and some cold ham and a pie. I tell you, George, there is that in this flight which makes me more than commonly angry."

George patted down the front of his silk flowered waistcoat. "No doubt, dear boy. I see I could not have called on a more untimely night. But since we have you so seldom in Truro these days I'm compelled to wait on you and mix duty with pleasure."

It reached Francis's taut and preoccupied mind that George was leading up to something. As his chief creditor George was in a dangerously powerful position; and feeling had not been too good between them since the gambling affray in April.

"An *agreeable* duty?"

"Well, it may be considered so. It has to do with Sanson and the matter you raised some time since."

So far neither Francis nor anyone else had got anything out of the miller. He had left Truro the day following Ross's exposure and was believed to be in

London. His mills, it turned out, belonged to a company and that company to other companies.

George took out his gold-mounted snuffbox and tapped it.

"We have talked this over several times, my father and I. While there's no obligation in it, Sanson's conduct is a stain we feel rather deeply. As you know, we have no ancestors to bring us repute; we must make our own."

"Yes, yes, you are clear enough," Francis said briefly. It was seldom that George mentioned his humble beginnings.

"Well, as I told you in May, many of your bills given to Matthew Sanson have found their way into Cary's hands. He has always been somewhat the treasurer of the family, as Matthew was the black sheep, and your bills were accepted by Cary in exchange for cash advances made to Matthew."

Francis grunted. "I take that as no advantage."

"Well, yes, it is. We have decided between us as a family to cancel one half of all the drafts which came into Cary's hands from Matthew. It will not be a crushing matter, but it will be a token of our will to undo what wrong has been done. As I say, not a big thing. About twelve hundred pounds."

Francis flushed. "I can't take your charity, George."

"Charity be hanged. You may have lost the money unfairly in the first place. From our viewpoint we wish it, to reestablish our integrity. It is really nothing at all to do with you."

Mrs. Tabb came in with the supper. She set up a table by the window, put her tray on it and two chairs beside it. Francis watched her. Half his mind was still battling with the desertion of Verity, the perfidy of Ross — the other half facing this princely gesture from a man he had begun to distrust. It *was* a princely gesture and one that no stubborn prickly pride must force him to refuse.

When Mrs. Tabb had gone he said: "You mean — the money would be put to reducing my debt to you?"

"That's for you to decide. But I'd suggest one half of it should go to reducing the debt and the other half should be a cash payment.''

Francis's flush deepened. ''It is very handsome of you. I don't know quite what to say.''

''Say nothing more about it. It's not a comfortable subject between friends, but I had to explain.''

Francis dropped into his chair. ''Take some supper, George. I'll open a bottle of my father's brandy after, in honour of the occasion. No doubt it will loosen up my anger over Verity and make me a more easy companion. You'll stay the night?''

''Thank you,'' said George.

They supped.

In the winter parlour Elizabeth had just excused herself and left again. Mr. Odgers was finishing up the raspberry syllabub and Mrs. Odgers the almond cake. With only the old lady's eyes on them their manners had eased up.

''I wonder if he means to do the honest thing by her,'' Mrs. Odgers said. ''They could not get married to-night, and you never can tell with these sailors. He may well have a Portugee wife for all she knows. What do you think, Clarence?"

"Um?" said Mr. Odgers, with his mouth full.

"Little Verity," said Aunt Agatha. "Little Verity. Imagine little Verity going off like that."

"I wonder what the feeling will be in Falmouth," said Mrs. Odgers. "Of course in a port morals are always more lax. And they may go through some marriage ceremony just to pull the wool over people's eyes. Anyway, men who kill their first wives should be forbidden ever to marry again. Don't you agree, Clarence?"

"Um," said Mr. Odgers.

"Little Verity," said Aunt Agatha. "She was always obstinate like her mother. I bring to mind when she was six or seven, the year we held the masquerade ball . . ."

In the large parlour the brandy had come.

"I can't bear these sneaking underhand dealings," Francis said bitterly. "If he had had the guts to come here and face me out maybe I should not have liked that, but I shouldn't have held him in such

552

contempt." After his estrangement from George the reaction was carrying him back beyond the old intimacy. As good as in his pocket was six hundred pounds he had never thought to see again — and the same amount cut from his debts. Never could it have been more welcome than to-day. During the coming months it might just make all the difference. It meant an easing of their life and the strain of bitter economy. A grand gesture which deserved the grand recognition. Adversity showed up one's friends.

"But all along," he continued, "that has been his way. At the outset he went sneaking behind our backs and meeting the girl at Nampara — with Ross's connivance. All the time it has been this sneaking, sneaking. I've half a mind to ride to Falmouth to-morrow and flush them from their love nest."

"And no doubt you'd find he had just left for Lisbon and she with him." George tasted the brandy on his lips. "No, Francis, leave them be. It is no good putting yourself in the wrong by trying to force her to return. The harm is done.

Maybe she'll soon be crying to come back."

Francis got up and began to light the candles. "Well, she shall not come back here, not if she cries for a year! Let her go to Nampara, where they have fathered this thing. Damn them, George." Francis turned, the taper showing up his angry face. "If there is one thing in this that cuts me to the root it is Ross's cursed underhand interference. Damn it, I might have expected a greater loyalty and friendship from my only cousin! What have I ever done to him that he should go behind my back in this fashion!"

"Well," said George, "I suppose you married the girl he wanted, didn't you?"

Francis stopped again and stared at him. "Oh, yes. Oh, yes . . . But that's long ago." He blew out the taper. "That was patched up long since. He is happily married himself; more happily than . . . There would be no point in feeling a grudge on that score."

George looked out on the darkening garden. The candles threw his blurred hunched shadow on the wall.

"You know Ross better than I, Francis, so I can't guide you. But many people — many people we accept on their face value have strange depths. I've found it so. It may be that Ross is one such. I can't judge but I do know that all my own overtures towards him have met with rebuffs."

Francis came back to the table. "Aren't you on friendly terms? No, I suppose not. How have you offended him?"

"That's something I can't guess. But I do know when his mine was opened all the other venturers were for the business being put through our bank, yet he fought tooth and nail until he got them to accept Pascoe's. Then sometimes remarks he has made have been repeated to me; they were the words of a man with a secret resentment. Finally there is this wildcat scheme he has launched of some copper-smelting company, which privately is directed at us."

"Oh, I don't think exactly at you," Francis. "Its aim is to get fairer prices for the mines."

George glanced covertly at him. "I'm

not at all upset about it, for the scheme will fail through lack of money. Still, it shows an enmity towards me which I don't feel I deserve — any more than you deserve to have had this betrayal of the best interests of your family."

Francis stared down at the other man, and there was a long silence. The clock in the corner struck seven.

"I don't think the scheme need necessarily fail through lack of money," Francis said whitely. "There are a good many important interests behind it. . . ."

CHAPTER III

It was an easterly sky, and as they reached Falmouth the sun was setting like a Chinese lantern, swollen and crimson and monstrous and decorated with ridges of curly cloud. The town was a grey smudge climbing the edge of the bay.

As they went down the hill Andrew said: "Your last letter left all to me, my dear; so I trust what I have done you'll find to your liking."

"I'm willing to do whatever you say."

"The wedding is set for eleven to-morrow — at the church of King Charles the Martyr. I took a licence from Parson Freakes yesterday morning. Just my old landlady and Captain Brigg will be there as witnesses. It will be as quiet as ever possible."

"Thank you."

"As for to-night, I had thought at first the best would be to take a room at one of the inns. But as I went round they all seemed too shoddy to house you."

"I shall not mind."

"I misliked the thought of you being there alone with perhaps noisy and drunken men about." His blue eyes met hers. "It wasn't right."

She flushed. "It wouldn't have mattered."

"So instead I'd like you to go to your new home, where Mrs. Stevens will be there to see to your needs. I'll sleep in my ship."

She said: "Forgive me if I seem listless . . . It isn't that at all. It's only the wrench of leaving the things I've loved so long."

"My dear, I know how you must feel. But we have a week before I need sail. I believe it will all seem different to you before I go."

Another silence fell. "Francis is unpredictable," she said suddenly. "In some ways, though I shall miss them so much, I wish we were further than a score of miles. It is within too-easy riding distance of some quarrelsome impulse."

"If he comes I will soon cool it for him."

"I know, Andrew. But that is above all what I don't want."

He smiled slightly. "I was very patient at the Assembly. At need I can be patient again."

Sea gulls were flying and crying. The smell of the sea was different from home, tanged with salt and seaweed and fish. The sun set before they reached the narrow main street, and the harbour was brimming with the limpid colours of the afterglow.

People, she thought, stared at them. No doubt he was a well-known figure in the town. Would the prejudice be very strong against him? If any remained, then it was her task to break it down. There could clearly be none against her.

She glanced sidelong at him, and the thought came into her head that they had met not three dozen times in all their lives. Had she things to face that she knew nothing of? Well, if they loved each other there was no other consideration big enough to stand beside it.

They stopped and he helped her down and they went into the porticoed house. Mrs. Stevens was at the door and greeted Verity pleasantly enough, though not without a trace of speculation and jealousy.

Verity was shown the dining-room and kitchen on the ground floor, the graceful parlour and bedroom on the first floor, the two attic bedrooms above, which were for the children when they were home, these children she had never seen. Esther, sixteen, was being educated by relatives; James, fifteen, a midshipman in the Navy. Verity had had so much opposition to face at home that she had hardly yet had time to consider the opposition she might find here.

Back in the parlour Andrew was standing looking out across the glimmering colours of the harbour. He turned as she came and stood beside him at the window. He took her hand. The gesture brought comfort.

"Which is your ship, Andrew?"

"She's well back from here, in St. Just's Pool. The tallest of the three. I doubt if you can make her out in this light."

"Oh, yes, she looks beautiful. Can I see over her sometime?"

"To-morrow if you wish." She suddenly felt his happiness. "Verity, I'll go now. I have asked Mrs. Stevens to serve your supper as soon as she can. You'll be tired from your ride and will not mind being quiet."

"Can you not stay to supper?"

He hesitated. "If you wish it."

"Please. What a lovely harbour this is! I shall be able to sit here and see all the shipping go in and out and watch for your coming home."

In a few minutes they went down into the little dining-room and ate boiled neck of mutton with capers, and raspberries and cream. An hour ago they had been very adult, making a rash gesture with strange caution, as if unable quite to free themselves of the restraints and hesitations grown with the years. But the candlelight loosed thoughts, softened doubts and discovered pride in their adventure.

They had never had a meal together before.

Net curtains were drawn across the windows, and figures crossed and recrossed them in the street outside. In the room they were a little below the level of the cobbles, and when a cart rumbled past the wheels were more visible than the driver.

They began to talk about his ship, and he told her of Lisbon, its chiming bells, the endless blazing sunlight, the unbelievable filth of the streets, the orange trees, the olive groves. Sometime she must go with him. Was she a good sailor?

She nodded eagerly, never having been to sea.

They laughed together, and a clock in the town began to strike ten. He got up.

''This is disgraceful, love. Compromising in the eyes of Mrs. Stevens, I'm sure. She'll expect us to have eaten all her cakes.''

She said: "If you had gone before I should have felt very strange here alone."

His self-disciplined face was unguarded

just then. "Last night I closed a book on my old life, Verity. To-morrow we'll open a new one. We must write it together."

"That's what I want," she said. "I'm not at all afraid."

He walked to the door, and then glanced at her still sitting at the table. He came back.

"Good night."

He bent to kiss her cheek, but she offered him her lips. They stayed so; and his hand on the table came up and lay on her shoulder.

"If ill comes to you, Verity, it will not be my doing. I swear it. Good night, love."

"Good night, Andrew, my love, good night."

He broke away and left her. She heard him run upstairs for his hat and then come down again and go out. She saw him pass the window. She stayed there for a very long time, her eyes half closed and her head resting against the high-backed chair.

CHAPTER IV

At about the time Verity was climbing the stairs with a candle to sleep in her new bed, Mark Daniel was taking up his pitch in Wheal Leisure Mine.

With him was one of the younger Martin boys, Matthew Mark, who was there to help him by carrying away the "dead" ground as he picked it and dumping it in a pit in the near-by cave. The air was so bad in here that their hempen candles would not burn properly; so that they worked in more than half darkness. The walls of the tunnel streamed with moisture and there was water and slush underfoot. But Matthew Mark thought himself lucky to work for so experienced a man for sixpence a day — or night — and he was learning fast. In another few years he would be bidding for a pitch of his own.

Mark never had much to say when he was working, but to-night he had not spoken a word. The boy did not know what was wrong and was afraid to ask. Being only just nine, he might not have understood quite what was gnawing at his companion even if he had been told.

For days now Mark had given up trying to believe there was nothing wrong. For weeks he had known in his heart but had said no to himself. The little signs had piled up, the hints from those who knew and did not dare, the sly glances; small by themselves, they had grown like snowflakes on a roof, weight to weight, until the roof crashed in.

He knew now, and he knew who.

She had been clever. He had always looked for signs of a man in the cottage but had never found any. He had tried to catch her out, but always she thought ahead of him. Her wits moved quick. The snow leopard was sharper than the black bear.

But in the wet weather of last week she had not been so clever. The ground had been so soft that even though she kept to the stony places there were marks here and there of her feet.

He dreaded this week of nightwork because it would bring him to some climax. The fear he felt in breaking out was because he could not shake his anger free from the clinging strands of his love. They still bound him; he struggled in a mesh with his grief.

The powder for blasting was needed now. He could go no farther with the pick. He said as much to Matthew and picked up his great hammer and the steel borer. With ease come from long practice he chose his place in the hard rock, drilled a deep hole in the face of the work, pulled out the borer and cleaned and dried the hole. Then he took up his case of powder and dropped powder in. Through the powder he pushed a tapering rod like an iron nail and filled up the mouth of the hole with clay, ramming it hard with his boring bar. This done, he pulled out the nail and into the thin hole threaded a hollow reed filled with powder, for a fuse.

He took off his hat, gently blew the smoky candle until it flickered into a flame and lit the reed. Then they both backed away round the first corner.

Mark counted twenty. Nothing. He counted another twenty. He counted fifty. Then he picked up his can and swore. In the darkness he had planted it against the wall and water had got into it.

"A misfire," he said.

"Have a care, Mr. Daniel," Matthew said. Blasting was the part of mining he did not like. "Give it a while."

But Mark had grunted and was already walking up to the charge. The boy followed.

As Mark drew out the reed there was a flash and a rumble and the rocks flew in his face. He put up hands to his eyes and fell back. The wall gave way.

The boy lost his head and turned and ran away, going for help. Then he checked himself and pushed his way through the choking black fumes to where Mark was trying to climb out from among the rocks.

He caught at his arm. "Mr. Daniel! Mr. Daniel!"

"Get back, boy! There's only a part gone."

But Matthew would not leave him and they groped their way to the bend in the tunnel.

Matthew blew on his candle, and in the flickering light stared at Mark. His gaunt face was black and striped with blood, his front hair and eyebrows singed.

"Your eyes, Mr. Daniel. Are they all right?"

Mark stared at the candle. "Aye, I can see." There was another roar in the tunnel as the rest of the charge went off. Black smoke billowed out and around them. "Take heed, boy, an' a warning that you always d'use the powder wi' a greaterer care."

"Your face. Thur's blood."

Mark stared down at his hands. "Tes these." His left hand was bleeding from the palms and fingers. The dampness of the powder had caused the accident but it had saved his life. He took out a dirty rag and wrapped it round his head.

"We'll wait till the fumes clear, an' then we'll see what it's brought down."

Matthew sat back on his heels and looked at the blood-streaked figure. "You did ought to see surgeon. He's proper with wounds an' things."

Mark got up sharply. "Nay. I'd not go to him if I was dying." He turned into the smoke.

They worked on for a time, but he found it hard to use his injured hand, which would not stop bleeding. His face was stinging and sore.

After an hour he said: "Reckon I'll go up to grass for a bit. You'd best come too, boy. There's no good breathin' this black air if you've no need."

Matthew followed him gladly enough. The nightwork tired him more than he would admit.

They reached the main shaft and climbed up it; the distance was nothing to Grambler and they were soon sniffing the fresh night air and hearing the rumble of the sea. There was a lovely biting sweetness in filling your lungs as you came up to grass. One or two men were about, and they clustered round Mark giving him advice.

He had come up to have a proper bandage put on and go below again. But as he stood there talking with the others and let his fingers be tied up, all the old trouble came back and he knew with angry panic that this was the moment for the test.

For a while he resisted, feeling it sprung on him too soon, that he had need to be prepared. Then he turned to Matthew and said:

"Run along home, boy. Twill be better for me not to go b'low again to-night."

When Matthew Mark was out and working he never let himself think of sleep — it didn't do — but now he was overwhelmed. It was little after midnight. A whole six extra hours in bed! He waited respectfully for a moment to walk part way home with Mark, but another gruff word sent him off in the direction of Mellin Cottages.

Mark saw him out of sight, then briefly bade good night to the other men and followed. He had told them he didn't know whether to bother Dr. Enys; but in fact his mind was quite made up. He knew just what he was going to do.

He walked quietly home. As the cottage

showed up in the starlight he felt his chest grow tight. He would have prayed if he had been a praying man, for his own mistake, for Keren's trueness, for a new life of trust. He came to the door, reached out for the latch, grasped it, pressed.

The door opened.

Breathe hard now and clumsily go in; he couldn't hold his breath, it panted away as if he'd been running for his life. No stop to make a light but pass through into the bedroom. Shutters were closed, and in the dark with unhurt hand grope a way round the walls of the cottage — his cottage — to the bed. The corner, the rough blanket. Sit on the edge and hand move over bed for Keren — his Keren. She was not there.

With a deep grunt of pain he sat there knowing this was the end. His breath was in sobs. He sat and panted and sobbed. Then he got up.

Out in the night again a pause to rub fingers over his eyes, to look right and left, to sniff, to set off for Mingoose.

The Gatehouse looked in darkness. He made a circle, sizing it up. A chink of light in an upper window.

Stop and stare and try to fight down the pain. It was in his blood, beating through him. The door of the house.

And there he stopped. To hammer to be let in would give warning. Time to think before they opened. She might slip out another way. They both thought so much quicker. They'd brazen it out. This time he must have proof.

I'll wait, he thought.

He crept slowly away, his long back bent, until he was just right to watch the front door or the back.

I'll crouch here and wait.

The stars moved up the sky, climbing and turning on their endless roundabout. A gentle wind stirred and sighed among the bracken and the brake, stirred and moved and then lay down again to sleep. A cricket began to saw among the gorse, and somewhere overhead a night-hawk cried: a ghostly sound, the spirit of a long-dead miner walking sightless over his old land. Small animals stirred in the undergrowth. An owl settled on the roof top and harshly cried.

I'll wait.

Then in the east a faint yellow light showed, and there crept up into the sky the wasted slip of an old moon. It hung there sere and dry, climbed a little, and then began to set.

The door of the Gatehouse opened a few inches and Keren slipped out.

For once she was happy. Happy that this was only the first night of Mark's night core. Their way — hers and Dwight's — was still strange, touched with things which had never been in her first thoughts. Possessive and a little jealous, she found herself forced to allow a division of his loyalty. His work was his first love. She had reached him by taking an interest in his work. She held him by maintaining it.

Not that she really minded. In a way she enjoyed playing the role of sober helpmeet. Something like her old part in *Hilary Tempest*. She sometimes dreamed of herself as his wife — Mark out of the way — wholly charming in a workmanlike but feminine dress, helping Dwight in some serious strait. Her hands, she knew, would be cool and capable, her manner superbly helpful; he would be full of admiration for her afterwards; and not only he but all the gentry of the countryside. She would be talked of everywhere. She had heard all about Mistress Poldark having been a great success at the celebration ball, and quite a number of people had been riding over to see her since then. Keren could not think why.

It had gone to her head, for she'd thought fit last month to come the lady and drop a hint to Keren about being careful what she did; and Keren had resented it. Well, if she were so successful in society, Keren, as a doctor's wife, would go much further. She might not even stay a doctor's wife all her life. There was no limit to what might happen. A big, hairy elderly man, who had been over to the Poldarks' one day, had met her as she crossed Nampara Combe, and he had given her more than a moment's look. When she knew he was a baronet and unmarried she'd been thankful for wearing that flimsy frock.

She ploughed through the rough undergrowth on her way back to the cottage. It had been the half after three by Dwight's clock, so there was nice time. As well not to run it too close. A mist had settled on the low ground between the two houses. She plunged into it as into a stream. Things were hung heavy with moisture; the damp touched her face and glistened on her hair. Some moonflowers showed among the scrub, and she picked one as she passed. She groped across the gully, climbed again and came out into the crystal-cool air.

So to-night as she lay naked in Dwight's arms she had encouraged him to talk: about the work of the day, about the little boy who had died of the malignant sore throat over at Marasanvose, about the results of his treatment on a woman in bed with an abscess, about his thoughts for the future. All this was like a cement to their passion. It had to be, with him. She did not really mind.

The moon was setting as she reached the cottage, and dawn was blueing the east. Back the way she had come the gully was as if filled with a stream of milk. Everywhere else was clear.

She went in and turned to close the door. But as she did so a hand from outside came to press it open. "Keren."

Her heart stopped; and then it began to bang. It banged till it mounted to her head and seemed to split.

"Mark!" she whispered. "You're home early. Is anything wrong?"

"Keren . . ."

"How dare you come startling me like this! I nearly died!"

Already she was thinking ahead of him, moving to attack and defeat his attack. But this time he had more than words to go on.

"Where've you been, Keren?"

"I?" she said. "I couldn't sleep. I have had a pain. Oh, Mark, I had such a terrible pain. I cried for you. I thought perhaps you could have made me something warm to send it better. But I was all alone. I didn't know what to do. So I thought maybe a walk would help. If I'd known you was coming home early I'd have come to the mine to meet you." In the half-dark her sharp eyes caught sight of the bandage on his hand. "Oh, Mark, you're hurt! There's been an accident. Let me see!"

She moved to him, and he struck her in the mouth with his burnt hand, knocked her back across the room. She fell in a small injured heap.

"Ye dirty liar! Ye dirty liar!" His breath was coming in sobs again.

She wept with her hurt. A strange, kittenish, girlish weeping, so far from his own.

He moved over to her. "Ye've been wi' Enys," he said in a terrible voice.

She raised her head. "Dirty yourself! Dirty coward! Striking a woman. Filthy beast! Get away from me! Leave me alone. I'll have you sent to prison, you! Get out!"

A faint light was coming in from the glimmering dawn; it fell on his singed and blackened face. Through the screen of her hands and hair she saw him, and at the sight she began to cry out.

"You've been wi' Enys, lying wi' Enys!" His voice climbed in great strides.

"I've not! I've not!" she screamed.

"Liar yourself! I went to see him about my pain. He's a doctor, ain't he? You filthy brute. I was in such pain."

Even now the quick-thoughted lie gave him pause. Above all things he had always wanted to be fair, to do the right thing by her.

"How long was you there?"

"Oh . . . over an hour. He gave me something to take an' then had to wait an——"

He said: "I waited more'n three."

She knew then that she must go and go quickly.

"Mark," she said desperately, "it isn't what you think. I swear before God it isn't. If you see him he'll explain. Let's go to him. Mark, he wouldn't leave me alone. He was always pestering me. Always and all the time. And then when once I yielded he threatened he'd tell you if I didn't go on. I swear it before God and my mother's memory. I hate him, Mark! I love only you! Go kill him if you want. He deserves it, Mark! I swear before God he took advantage of me!"

She went on, babbling at him, throwing

words at him, any words, pebbles at a giant, her only defence. She sprayed words, keeping his great anger away from her, twisting her brain this way and that. Then when she saw that it was going to avail no longer she sprang like a cat under his arm, leapt for the door.

He thrust out one great hand and caught her by the hair, hauled her screaming back into his arms.

She fought with all strength in her power, kicking, biting, scratching. He pushed her nails away from his eyes, accepting her bites as if they were no part of him. He pulled the cloth away from her throat, gripped it.

Her screaming stopped. Her eyes started tears, died, grew big. She knew there was death; but life called her, sweet life, all the sweet of youth, not yet gone. Dwight, the baronet, years of triumph, crying, dying.

She twisted and upset him and they fell against the shutter, whose flimsy catch gave way. They leaned together out of the window, she beneath him.

A summer morning. The glazing eyes of

the girl he loved, the woman he hated; her face swollen now. Sickened, mad, his tears dropped on her face.

Loose his hold, but her beautiful face still stared. Cover it with a great hand, push it away, back.

Under his hand, coming from under his hand, a faint gentle click.

He fell back upon the floor of the cottage, groping, moaning upon the floor.

But she did not move.

There was no cloud in the sky. There was no wind. Birds were chirping and chattering. Of the second brood of young thrushes which Mark had watched hatch out in the stunted hawthorn tree only a timid one stayed; the others were out fluttering their feathers, shaking their heads, sharp with incentive, eyeing this strange new world.

The ribbon of milky mist still lay in the gully. It stretched down to the sea, and there were patches across the sand hills like steam from a kettle.

When light came full the sea was calm, and there seemed nothing to explain the roar in the night. The water was a pigeon's-egg blue with a dull terra-cotta haze above the horizon and a few pale carmine tips where the rising sun caught the ripples at the sand's edge.

The ugly shacks of Wheal Leisure were clear-cut, and a few men moving about them in their drab clothes looked pink and handsome in the early light.

The mist stirred before the sun's rays, quickened with the warmth and melted and moved off to the low cliffs, where it crouched in the shade for a while before being thrust up and away.

A robin that Keren and Mark had tamed fluttered down to the open door, puffed out his little chest and hopped inside. But although the cottage was silent he did not like the silence, and after pecking here and there for a moment he hopped out. Then he saw one of his friends leaning out of the window, but she made no welcoming sound and he flew away.

The sun fell in at the cottage, strayed across the sanded floor, which was pitted and scraped with the marks of feet. A tinderbox lay among the sand, and the stump of a candle, a miner's hat beside an upturned chair.

The moonflower Keren had picked lay on the threshold. Its head had been broken in the struggle but the petals were still white and damp with a freshness that would soon begin to fade.

CHAPTER V

Ross had been dreaming that he was arguing about the smelting works with Sir John Trevaunance and the other shareholders. It was not an uncommon dream or one which went by contraries. Half his waking life was made up of defending the Carnmore Copper Company from inward fission or outside attack. For the battle was carefully joined, and no one could tell which way it would go.

Nothing much was barred in this struggle. Pressure had been brought to bear on United Mines, and Richard Tonkin had been forced out of the managership. Sir John Trevaunance had a lawsuit dragging on in Swansea over his coal ships.

Ross dreamed there was a meeting at Trevaunance's home, as there was to be in a few days, and that everyone was quarrelling at once. He pounded the table again and again trying to gain a hearing. But no one would listen and the more he pounded the more they talked, until suddenly everyone fell silent and abruptly he found himself awake in the silent room and listening to the knocking on the front door.

It was quite light and the sun was falling across the half-curtained windows. The Gimletts should be up soon. He reached for his watch but as usual had forgotten to wind it. Demelza's dark hair clouded the pillow beside him, and her breathing came in a faint *tic-tic.* She was always a good sleeper; if Julia woke she would be out and about and asleep again in five minutes.

Hasty footsteps went downstairs and the knocking stopped. He slid out of bed and Demelza sat up, as usual wide-awake, as if she had never been asleep at all.

"What is it?"

"I don't know, my dear."

There was a knock on the door and Ross opened it. Somehow in such emergencies he still expected to see Jud standing there.

"If you please, sur," said Gimlett, "a boy wants to see you. Charlie Baragwanath, who's gardener's boy over to Mingoose. He's terrible upset."

"I'll be down."

Demelza breathed a quiet sigh into the bedclothes. She had thought it something about Verity. All yesterday, lovely yesterday, of which they had spent a good part on the beach in the sun paddling their feet in the sun-warmed water, all the time she had thought of Verity. It had been Verity's day of release, for which she, Demelza, had plotted and schemed for more than a year. She had wondered and waited.

With only her eyes showing over the rim of the bedclothes she watched Ross dress and go down. She wished people would leave them alone. All she wanted was to be left alone with Ross and Julia. But people came more, especially her suitors, as Ross satirically called them. Sir Hugh Bodrugan had been several times to tea.

Ross came back. She could tell at once that something was wrong.

"What is it?"

"Hard to get sense out of the boy. I believe it is something at the mine."

She sat up. "An accident?"

"No. Go to sleep for a little. It is not much after five."

He went down again and joined the undersized boy, whose teeth were chattering as if with cold. He gave him a sip or two of brandy and they set off through the apple trees over the hill.

"Were you first there?" Ross asked.

"Aye, sur . . . I — I b'long to call that way on my way over. Not as they're always about not at this time o' year when I'm s'early; but I always b'long to go that tway. I thought they was all out. An' then I seen 'er . . . an' then I seen 'er. . . ."

He covered his face with his hands.

"Honest, sur, I near fainted away. I near fell away on the spot."

As they neared the cottage they saw three men standing outside. Paul Daniel and Zacky Martin and Nick Vigus.

Ross said: "Is it as the boy says?"

Zacky nodded.

"Is anyone . . . inside?"

"No, sur."

"Does anyone know where Mark is?"

"No, sur."

"Have you sent for Dr. Enys?"

"Just sent, sur."

"Aye, we've sent fur he, sure 'nough," said Paul Daniel bitterly. Ross glanced at him.

"Will you come in with me, Zacky?" he said.

They went to the open door together, then Ross stooped his head and went in.

She was lying on the floor covered with a blanket. The sun from the window streamed across the blanket in a golden flood.

"The boy said . . ."

"Yes . . . We moved 'er. It didn't seem decent to leave the poor creature."

Ross knelt and lifted back the blanket. She was wearing the scarlet kerchief Mark had won at the wrestling match twenty months before. He put back the blanket, rose, wiped his hands.

"Zacky, where was Mark when this happened?" He said it in an undertone, as if not to be overheard.

"He should have been down the mine, Cap'n Ross, should by rights have been coming up now. But he had an accident early on his core. Matthew Mark was home to bed before one. Nobody has seen Mark Daniel since then."

"Have you any idea where he is?"

"That I couldn't say."

"Have you sent for the parish constable?"

"Who? Old Vage? Did we oughter have done?"

"No, this is Jenkins's business. This is Mingoose Parish."

A shadow fell across the room. It was Dwight Enys. The only colour in his face was in the eyes, which seemed suffused, as in a fever. "I . . ." He glanced at Ross, then at the figure on the floor. "I came . . ."

"A damned nasty business, Dwight." Friendship made Ross turn away from the young man towards Paul Daniel, who had followed him in. "Come, we should leave Dr. Enys alone while he makes his examination."

Paul seemed ready to challenge this;

but Ross had just too much authority to be set aside, and presently they were all out in the sun. Ross glanced back and saw Dwight stoop to move the cloth. His hand was trembling and he looked as if he might fall across the body in a faint.

All that day there was no word of Mark Daniel. Blackened and hurt, he had come up from the mine at midnight, and in the early hours of Monday morning had put his stamp upon unfaithfulness and deceit. Then the warm day had taken him.

So much everyone knew. For like the quiet movement of wind among grass, the whisper of Keren's deceit had spread through villages and hamlets round, and no one doubted that this had brought her death. And curiously, no one seemed to doubt the justice of the end. It was the Biblical punishment. From the moment she came here she had flaunted her body at other men. One other man, and they knew Who, had fallen into her lure. Any woman with half an eye would have known that Mark Daniel was not to be cuckolded lightly. She had known the risk and taken it, matching her sharp wits against his slow strength. For a time she had gone on and then she had made a slip and that had been the end. It might not be law but it was justice.

And the Man in the case might thank his stars he too wasn't laid across the floor with a broken neck. He might yet find himself that way if he didn't watch out. If they were in his shoes they'd get on a horse and ride twenty miles and stay away while Mark Daniel was at large. For all his scholaring he was not much more than a slip of a boy, and Daniel could snap him as easy as a twig.

There wasn't much feeling against him, as there might well have been. In the months he had been here they had grown to like him, to respect him, where they all disliked Keren. They might have risen against him as a breaker of homes; but instead they saw Keren as the temptress who had led him away. Many a wife had seen Keren look at *her* man. It wasn't the surgeon's fault, they said. But all the same they wouldn't be in *his* shoes. He'd had to go in and examine the body, and it was said that when he came out the sweat was pouring off his face.

At six that evening Ross went to see Dwight.

At first Bone would not admit him; Doctor had said in no circumstances was he to be disturbed. But Ross pushed him aside.

Dwight was sitting at a table with a pile of papers before him and a look of hopeless despair on his face. He hadn't changed his clothes since this morning and he hadn't shaved. He glanced at Ross and got up.

"Is it something important?"

"There's no news. That's what is important, Dwight. If I were you I should not stay here until nightfall. Go and spend a few days with the Pascoes."

"What for?" he asked stupidly.

"Because Mark Daniel is a dangerous man. D'you think if he chose to seek you out Bone or a few locked doors would stop him?"

Dwight put his hands to his face. "So the truth is known everywhere."

"Enough to go on. One can do nothing in

private in a country district. For the time being——"

He said: "I'll never forget her face! Two hours before I'd been kissing it!"

Ross went across and poured him a glass of brandy.

"Drink this. You're lucky to be alive and we must keep you so."

"I fail to see any good reason."

Ross checked himself. "Listen, boy," he said more urgently, "you must take a good hold on yourself. This thing is done and can't be undone. What I wish above all is to prevent more mischief. I'm not here to judge you."

"I know," said the young man. "I know, Ross. I only judge myself."

"And that, no doubt, too harshly. Anyone sees that this tragedy has been of the girl's making. I don't know how much you came to feel for her."

Dwight broke down. "I don't know myself, Ross. I don't know. When I saw her lying there, I — I thought I had loved her."

Ross poured himself a drink. When he came back Dwight had partly recovered.

"The great thing is to get away for a time. Just for a week or so. The magistrates have issued a warrant for Mark's arrest, and the constables are out. That is all that can be done for the moment and it may be enough. But if Mark wants to evade capture I'm sure it will not be enough, because although every villager is bound by law to help in his capture, I don't believe one of them will raise a hand."

"They take his side, and rightly so."

"But not against you, Dwight. However, in a day or two other measures may be taken, and in a week Mark should be put away and it should be safe for you to return."

Dwight got up, rocking his half-empty glass.

"No, Ross! What d'you take me for! To skulk away in a safe place while the man is tracked down and then to come slinking back! I'd sooner meet him at once and take the outcome." He began to walk up and down the room. Then he came to a stop. "See it my way. On all counts I've let these people down. I came among then a stranger and a physician. I have met with nothing worse than suspicion and much that's been better than kindness. Eggs that could be ill spared pressed on me in return for some fanciful favour. Little gestures of good will even from people who are Choake's people. Confidence and trust. In return I have helped to break up the life of one of their number. If I went now I should go for good, a cheat and a failure."

Ross said nothing.

"But the other way and the harder way is to see this thing out and to take my chance. Look, Ross, there is another case of sore throat at Marasanvose. There is a woman with child at Grambler who nearly died last time with the ill management of a midwife. There are four cases of miner's consumption which are improving under treatment. There are people here and there trusting on me. Well, I've betrayed them; but it would be a greater betrayal to leave now — to leave them to Thomas Choake's farmyard methods."

"I was not saying you should."

Dwight shook his head. "The other's impossible."

"Then spend a few days with us. We have a room. Bring your man."

"No. Thank you for your kindness. From to-morrow morning I go about as usual."

Ross stared at him grimly. "Then your blood be on your own head."

Dwight put his hand up to his eyes. "Keren's blood is already there."

From the Gatehouse, Ross went direct to the Daniels. They were all sitting round in the half gloom of the cottage doing nothing. They were like mourners at a wake. All the adult family was present except Beth, Paul's wife, who was sharing Keren's lonely vigil in the cottage over the hill. Despised by Keren in life, Beth could yet not bear the thought of allowing her to lie untended all through the summer evening.

Old Man Daniel was sucking his clay pipe and talking, talking. Nobody seemed to listen; the old man didn't seem to care. He was trying to talk his grief and anxiety out of himself.

"I well call to mind when I was on Lake Superior in 'sixty-nine thur were a case not mislike this'n. On Lake Superior in 'sixty-nine — or were it 'seventy? — a man runned off wi' the storekeeper's woman. I well call it to mind. But twur through no fault——"

They greeted Ross respectfully, Grannie Daniel hopping tearfully off her shaky stool and inviting him to sit down. Ross was always very polite to Grannie Daniel, and she always tried to return it in kind. He thanked her and refused, saying he wanted a word in private with Paul.

"Twur through no fault of 'is. A man runned off wi' the storekeeper's woman, an' he plucked out a spade an' went arter 'em. Just wi' a spade. Nought else but a spade."

Paul straightened up his back and quietly followed Ross out into the sun. Then he closed the door and stood a little defensively with his back against it. There were other people about, standing at the doors of their cottages and talking, but they were out of earshot. "No news of Mark?"

"No, sur."

"Have you an idea where he could be?"

"No, sur."

"I suppose Jenkins has questioned you?"

"Yes, sur. And others in Mellin. But we don't know nothing."

"Nor would you tell anything if you did know, eh?"

Paul looked at his feet. "That's as may be."

"This is a different crime from petty theft, Paul. If Mark had been caught stealing something from a shop he might be transported for it; but if he hid for a time it might be forgotten. Not so with murder."

"How do we know he done it, sur?"

"If he did not, why has he fled?"

Paul shrugged his big shoulders and narrowed his eyes at the declining sun.

"Perhaps I should tell you what is likely to happen, Paul. The magistrates have issued a warrant and sent out the constable. Old blacksmith Jenkins from Marasanvose will do his best and Vage from Sawle will help too. I don't think they'll be successful."

"Maybe not."

"The magistrates will then organize a search. A man hunt is a very ugly thing. It should be avoided."

Paul Daniel shifted but did not speak.

Ross said: "I have known Mark since I was a boy, Paul. I should be unhappy to think of him hunted down perhaps with dogs and later swinging on a gibbet."

" 'E'll swing on a gibbet if he gives his self up," Paul said.

"Do you known where he is?"

"I don't know nothing. But I can 'ave me own ideas."

"Yes, indeed." Ross had found out what he wanted. "Listen, Paul. You know Nampara Cove? Of course. There are two caves. In one cave is a boat."

The other man looked up sharply. "Yes?"

"It is a small boat. One I use for fishing just around the coast. The oars I keep on a shelf at the back of the cave. The rowlocks are at home so that she shall not be used without my sanction."

Paul licked his lips. "Aye?"

"Aye. Also at home is a detachable mast and a pair of sails which can turn the boat into a cutter. She's a weatherly little craft, I know from experience. Not fit for ocean going when the seas are steep; but a resolute man could fare a lot worse in summer time. Now Mark is finished so far as England is concerned. But up in the north there's Ireland. And down in the south is France, where there's trouble at present. He has acquaintances in Brittany and he's made the crossing before."

"Aye?" said Paul, beginning to sweat.

"Aye," said Ross.

"An' what of the sails and the rullocks?"

"They might find their way down to the cave after dark. And a few bits of food to keep a man alive. It was just an idea."

Paul rubbed his forearm over his forehead. "Be thanked for the idea. Why if——"

"I make one condition," Ross said, tapping him on the chest with a long forefinger. "This is a secret between two or three. Being accessory to murder is not a pretty thing. I will not have the Viguses privy to it, for Nick has a slippery way of letting things escape him when they are to the detriment of others. There are those in authority who would find a greater relish in their meals if I ran my neck into a noose. Well, I don't intend to do that, not for you nor your brother nor all the broken hearts in Mellin. So you must go careful. Zacky Martin would help if you needed another outside your own family."

"Nay, I'll keep it to myself, sur. There's no need for others to be in on it. Twould kill the old man to see Mark swing — an' mebbe Old Grannie too, though there's no guessing what she'll survive like. But tes the disgrace of it. If so be——"

"Do you know where he is now?"

"I know where I can leave un a note; we used to play so as lads. But I reckon twill be to-morrow night 'fore anything can be done. First I've to fix a meetin', and then I've to persuade'n as tis best for all that he go. They d'say he's fair broke up with it all."

"Some have seen him then?"

Paul glanced quickly at the other man. "Aye."

"I don't think he will refuse to go if you mention his father. But make it urgent. It must be not later than to-morrow."

"Aye. I'll do that. If so be as it can be fixed for to-night I'll leave ee know. An' *thank* ee, sur. Them as don't know can't ever thank ee, but they would, fairly they would!"

Ross turned to walk back. Paul re-entered the cottage. Inside Old Man Daniel was going on just as if he had never stopped in his quavering, rusty voice, talking round and round to stop the silence from falling.

CHAPTER VI

Thoughtfully Ross walked back to Nampara. He found John Gimlett cleaning the windows of the library, for which Mrs. Gimlett had been making needlework curtains. The industry of the Gimletts, contrasting with sloth of the Paynters, always surprised him. The garden prospered. Last year Demelza had bought some hollyhock seeds, and in the windless summer they had coloured the walls of the house with their stately purples and crimsons. Julia lay in her cot in the shade of the trees and, seeing her awake, he walked across and picked her up. She crowed and laughed and clutched at his hair.

Demelza had been gardening, and Ross ran with Julia on his shoulder to meet her. She was in her white muslin dress and it gave him a queer twist of pleasure to see that she was wearing gloves. Gradually, without pretentiousness or haste, she was moving towards little refinements of habit.

She had matured this summer. The essential impish vitality of her would never alter, but it was more under her control. She had also grown to accept the startling fact that men found her worth pursuing.

Julia crowed with joy and Demelza took her from him.

"There is another tooth, Ross. See here. Put your finger just here. Is your finger clean? Yes, it will do. Now."

"Yes, indeed. She'll soon be able to bite like Garrick."

"Is there news of Mark?"

In an undertone Ross told her.

Demelza glanced at Gimlett. "Will it not be a great risk?"

"Not if it is done quick. I fancy Paul knows more than he has told me, and that Mark will come to-night."

"I am afraid for you. I should be afraid to tell anyone."

"I only hope Dwight will keep indoors until he is safe away."

"Oh, there is a letter for you from Elizabeth," Demelza said, as if she had just remembered.

She felt in her apron pocket and brought out the letter. Ross broke the seal.

Dear Ross *(it ran)*,

As you may know Verity left us last night for Captain Blamey. She left while we were at Evensong and has gone with him to Falmouth. They are to be married to-day.

Elizabeth

Ross said: "Well, so she has done it at last! I greatly feared she might."

Demelza read the letter.

"Why should they not be happy together? It is what I have always said, it is better to take a risk than mope away all your life in dull comfort and secureness."

"Why 'As you may know'? Why should she think I would know?"

"Perhaps it is already about."

Ross pushed back the hair Julia had

604

ruffled. It was an action which made him suddenly boyish. Yet his expression was not so.

"I do not fancy her life with Blamey. Yet you may be right in thinking she'll be happy with him. I pray she will." He released his other hand from Julia's clinging grasp. "It never rains but it pours. This means I must go to Trenwith and see them. The letter is abrupt in tone. I expect they are upset."

So it has all come, Demelza thought, and Verity by now is married to him, and I too pray they will be happy together, for if they are not I shall not be easy in my bed.

"It is less than an hour to sunset," Ross said. "I shall have to make haste." He looked at her. "I suppose you would not go and see them in my place?"

"Elizabeth and Francis? Judas, no! Oh, no, Ross. I would do a lot for you, but not that."

"I don't see that you need feel such alarm. But of course I must go. I wonder what at last brought Verity to the plunge — after all these years. I think also she might have left some letter for me."

When Ross had gone Demelza set Julia on her feet and allowed her to walk about the garden on her leading strings. She toddled here and there, crowing with delight and trying hard to get at the flowers. In the meantime Gimlett finished the windows and picked up his pail and went in, and Demelza thought her thoughts and watched the sun go down. It was not the sort of sunset one would have expected to follow the day; the sky was streaked and watery and the light faded quickly.

As the dew began to fall she picked up the child and carried her in. Gimlett had already taken in the cot and Mrs. Gimlett was lighting the candles. The Paynters' going had helped Demelza in her quest for ladyship.

She fed Julia on a bowl of bread and broth and saw her safely to sleep, and it was not till then that she realized Ross had been gone too long.

She went down the stairs and to the open front door. The fall of night had drawn a cloud across the sky, and a light cool wind moved among the trees. The weather was on the change. Over in the distance she caught the queer lap-dog bark of a moor hen.

Then she saw Ross coming through the trees.

Darkie neighed when she saw her at the door. Ross jumped off and looped the reins over the lilac tree.

"Has anyone been?"

"No. You've been a long time."

"I've seen Jenkins — also Will Nanfan, who always knows everything. Two other constables are to help Jenkins. Bring a candle, will you; I'd like to get those sails down at once."

She went with him into the library.

"The wind is rising. He must go to-night if it's at all possible. To-morrow may be too late for another reason."

"What's that, Ross?"

"Sir Hugh is one of the magistrates concerned, and he's pressing for calling in the military. Apparently she — Keren — apparently Sir Hugh had noticed her, seen her about, thought her attractive, you know what a lecherous old roué he is——"

"Yes, Ross. . . ."

"So he's taking a personal interest. Which is bad for Mark. He has another reason too."

"How is that?"

"You remember at St. Ann's last week when the Revenue man was mishandled. The authorities have sent out a troop of dragoons to-day to St. Ann's. They are to be stationed there for a time as a cautionary measure, and may make a search during their stay. Sir Hugh, as you know, is a friend of Mr. Trencrom and buys all his spirits there. It would not be unnatural to take attention from the smugglers for a day by asking help in a search for a murderer."

". . . Shall I come down to the cave with you?"

"No, I shall not be more than half an hour."

"And — Verity . . ."

Ross paused at the door of the library with the mast on his shoulder.

"Oh . . . Verity is gone sure enough. And I have had a fantastic quarrel with Francis."

"A quarrel?" She had sensed there was something else.

"In good measure. He taxed me with having arranged this elopement and even refused to believe me when I said not. I've never been so taken aback in my life. I gave him credit for some degree of — of intelligence."

Demelza moved suddenly, as if trying to shift the cold feeling that had settled on her.

"But, my dear . . . why you?"

"Oh, they thought I had been using you as a go-between; picking up his letters somewhere and getting you to deliver them to Verity. I could have knocked him down. Anyway, we have broken for a long time. There will not be any easy patching up after what has been said."

"Oh, Ross, I'm . . . that sorry . . . I . . ."

To hide his own discomfort he said lightly: "Now stay about somewhere while I'm gone. And tell Gimlett I'm back. It will occupy him to tend on Darkie."

So in a few minutes more she was alone

again. She had walked a little way along the stream with him and had watched his figure move into the dark. From this point you could hear the waves breaking in the cove.

Before she had been uneasy, a little nervy and anxious, for it was not pleasant to be helping a murderer to escape. But now her unhappiness was a different thing, solid and personal and settled firm, as if it would never move, for it touched the all-important matter of her relations with Ross. For a year she had worked untiringly for Verity's happiness, worked open-eyed, knowing that what she was doing would be condemned by Ross and doubly condemned by Francis and Elizabeth. But she had never imagined that it would cause a break between Ross and his cousin. That was something outside all sensible counting. She was desperately troubled.

So deep was she in this that she did not notice the figure coming across the lawn towards the door. She had turned in and was closing the door when a voice spoke. She stepped back behind the door so that the lantern in the hall shone out.

"Dr. Enys!"

"I hadn't thought to startle you, Mistress Poldark. . . . Is your husband in?"

Having begun to thump, Demelza's heart was not quieting yet. There was another kind of danger here.

"Not at the moment."

Her eyes took in his dishevelled look, so changed from the neat, comely, black-coated young man of ordinary times. He might have been without sleep for a week. He stood there indecisive, conscious that he had not been asked in, knowing something guarded in her attitude but mistaking the causes.

"Do you imagine he'll be long?"

"About half an hour."

He part turned away as if leaving. But there he stopped. "Perhaps you'll forgive me for intruding on you . . . ?"

"Of course."

She led the way into the parlour. There might be danger or there might not: she could not avoid it.

He stood there very stiffly. "Don't let

me interfere with anything you may be doing. I don't at all wish to interrupt you."

"No," she said in a soft voice, "I was doing nothing." She went across and drew the curtains, careful to leave no nicks. "As you'll see we are late with supper, but Ross has been busy. Would you take a glass of port?"

"Thank you, I won't. I . . ." As she turned from the window he said impulsively: "You condemn me for my part in this morning's tragedy?"

She coloured a little. "How can I condemn anyone when I know such a small bit about it?"

"I shouldn't have mentioned it. But I have been thinking — thinking all to-day and speaking to no one. To-night I felt I must come out, go out somewhere. And this house was the only one . . ."

She said: "It might be dangerous to be out to-night."

"I think highly of your opinion," he said. "Yours and Ross's. It was his confidence that brought me here; if I felt I had forfeited it, it would be better to cut and go."

"I don't think you've forfeited it. But I don't think he will be pleased by you coming here to-night."

"Why?"

"I should rather not explain that,"

"Do you mean you want me to go?"

"I b'lieve it would be better." She picked up a plate from the table and set it in another place.

He looked at her. "I must have some assurance of your friendship — in spite of all. Alone in the Gatehouse this evening I have come near to — near to . . ." He did not finish.

She met his eyes.

"Stay then, Dwight," she said. "Sit down and don't bother 'bout me."

He slumped in a chair, passed his hands across his face. While Demelza pottered about and went in and out of the room he talked in snatches, explaining, arguing. Two things were absent, self-pity and self-apology. He seemed to be trying to make out a case for Keren. It was as if he felt she was being harshly judged and could offer no defence. He must speak for Keren.

Then the third time she went from the room and came back he did not go on. She glanced at him and saw him sitting tense.

"What is it?"

"I thought I heard someone tapping at the window."

Demelza's heart stopped beating altogether; then she gulped it into motion again. "Oh, I know what that is. Don't you get up. I will see for it myself."

Before he could argue she went out into the hall, shutting the parlour door behind her. So it had come. As she had feared. Pray Ross would not be long. Just for the moment she had to handle the crisis alone.

She went to the hall door and peered out. The dim lantern light showed an empty lawn. Something moved by the lilac bush.

"Beg pardon, ma'am," said Paul Daniel.

Her glance met his; strayed beyond him.

"Captain Ross has just gone down to the cove. Is . . . anyone with you?"

He hesitated. "You know about un?"

"I know."

He gave a low whistle. A dim figure broke from the side of the house. Paul leaned behind Demelza and pulled the hall door half shut so that the light should not shine out.

Mark stood before them. His face was in the shadow but she could see the caverns of his eyes.

"Cap'n Ross is down in the cove," said Paul. "We'd best go down to 'im."

Demelza said: "Sometimes Bob Baragwanath and Bob Nanfan go fishing there at high tide."

"We'll wait by yonder apple trees," said Paul. "We'll be well able to see 'im from thur."

And well able to see anyone leave the house. "You'll be safer indoors. You'll — be safer in the library."

She pushed open the door and moved into the hall, but they drew back and whispered together. Paul said:

"Mark don't want to tie you folk up wi' this more'n he can. He'd better prefer to wait outside."

"No, Mark. It don't matter to us.

Come in at once!''

Paul entered the hall and after him Mark, bending his head to get in the doorway. Demelza had just time to take in the blisters on his forehead, the stone grey of his face, the bandaged hand, before she opened the door of the bedroom which led to the library. Then as she picked up the lantern to go in there was a movement at the other side of the hall. Their eyes flickered across to Dwight Enys standing in the threshold of the parlour.

CHAPTER VII

Silence swelled in the hall, and burst.

Paul Daniel had slammed the outer door.

He stood with his back to it. Mark, gaunt and monstrous, stood quite still, the veins growing thick and knotted in his neck and hands.

She moved then, turned on them both.

"Dwight, go back into the parlour. Go back at once! Mark, d'you hear me! Mark!" Her voice didn't sound like her own.

"So tes a bloody trap," said Mark.

She stood before him, slight and seeming small. "How dare you say that! Paul, have you no sense? Take him. This way, at once."

"You bastard, you," said Mark, looking over her head.

"You should have thought of that before," said Dwight. "Before you killed her."

"Damned slimy adulterer. Tradin' on your work. Foulin' the nests o' those you pertend to help."

"You should have come for me," Dwight said, "not broken a girl who couldn't defend herself."

"Yes, by God——"

Demelza moved between them as Mark stepped forward. Blindly he tried to brush her away, but instead of that she stood her ground and hammered him on the chest with her clenched fists. His eyes flickered, lingered, came down.

"D'you realize what this means to us?" she said, breathless, her eyes blazing. "We've done nothing. We're trying to help. Help you both. You'd fight and kill each other in *our* house, on *our* land. Have you no loyalty and — and friendship that stands for anything at all! What's brought you here to-night, Mark? Mebbe not the thought to save your own skin, but to save the disgrace for your father an' his family. Twould kill him. Well, which is most important to you, your father's life or this man's? Dwight, go back into the parlour *at once!*"

Dwight said: "I can't. If Daniel wants me I must stay."

"What's 'e doing 'ere?" said Paul to the girl.

Dwight said: "Mistress Poldark tried to drive me away."

"You bastard," said Mark again.

Demelza caught him by the arm as he was about to raise it. "In here. Else we shall have the servants coming and there'll be no secret at all."

He did not move an inch under her pressure. "There'll be no secret wi' him in the know. Come outside, Enys. I'll finish you there."

"Nay." Paul had been useless so far, but now he took a hand. "There's no sense in that, Mark. I think bad of the skunk, same as you, but twill finish everything if you fight him."

"Everything's finished already."

"It *isn't!*" cried Demelza. "It *isn't,* I tell you. Don't you see! Dr. Enys can't betray you without betraying us."

619

Dwight hesitated, every sort of different impulse clamouring. "I won't betray anyone," he said.

Mark spat out a harsh breath. "I'd as lief trust a snake."

Paul came up to him. "It is an ill meetin', Mark; but we can't do nothin' about en. Come, old dear, we must do what Mistress Poldark say."

Dwight put his hands up to his head. "I'll not betray you, Daniel. Three wrongs don't make a right any more than two. What you did to Keren is with your conscience, as — as my ill-doing is with mine."

Paul pushed Mark slowly towards the bedroom door. Abruptly Mark shook off his arm and stopped again. His gaunt terrible face worked for a moment.

"Mebbe this ain't the time for a reckoning, Enys. But it will come, never fear."

Dwight did not raise his head.

Mark looked down at Demelza, who was still standing like a guardian angel between him and his wrath. "Nay, ma'am, I'll not stain your floor with more blood. I'd not wish hurt to this 'ouse. . . . Where d'you want for me to go?''

. . . When Ross came back Dwight was in the parlour, his head buried in his hands. Mark and Paul were in the library, Mark every now and then shaking with a spasm of anger. In the hall, between them, Demelza stood sentinel. When she saw Ross she sat down in the nearest chair and burst into tears.

"What the Devil . . . ?'' said Ross.

She spoke a few disjointed words.

He put the sail down in the corner of the hall.

" . . . Where are they now? And you . . .''

She shook her head and pointed.

He came over to her. "And there's been no bloodletting? My God, I'll swear it has never been nearer. . . .''

"You may swear it in truth," Demelza said.

He put his arm about her. "Did you stop it, love? Tell me, how did you stop it?''

"Why have you brought the sail back?'' she asked.

"Because there'll be no sailing yet. The

swell has got up with the tide. It would overturn the boat before we ever could get her launched."

An hour before dawn they went down to the cove, following the bubble of the stream and the descending combe, with a glowworm here and there green-lit like a jewel in the dark. The tide had gone out but the swell was still heavy, rushing in and roaring at them whenever they got too near. That was the trouble with the north coast: a sea could get up without warning and then you were done.

In the first glimmerings of daybreak, with the deathly moon merging its last candlelight in the blueing east, they walked slowly back. Twenty-four hours ago there had been a terrible anger in Mark's soul, bitter and blighting and hot; now all feeling was dead. His black eyes had sunk deeply into the frame of his face.

As they neared the house he said: "I'll be gettin' on my way."

Ross said: "We'll house you here till to-morrow."

"No. I'll not have ye into it more."

Ross stopped. "Listen, man. The country folk are on your side, but you'll bring trouble on them if you shelter among 'em. You'll be safe in the library. To-night may be calm enough, for no wind is up."

"That man may tell about you," said Paul Daniel.

"Who? Enys? No, you do him an injustice there."

They went on again.

"Look, mister," said Mark, "I don't concern whether I hang or fly. Nothing don't matter a snap to me now. But one thing I'm danged sure on is that I'll not skulk where I bring trouble to them as friends me. An' that's for sartin. Ef the soldiers d'come, well, let 'em come."

They reached the house in silence.

"You always were a stubborn mule," Ross said.

Paul said: "Now look ee here, Mark. I've the thought——"

Someone came out of the house.

"Oh, Demelza," Ross said in half irritation, "I told you to go to bed. There's no need to worry yourself."

"I've brewed a dish of tea. I thought you'd all be back about now."

They went into the parlour. By the light of a single candle Demelza poured them hot tea from a great pewter pot. The three men stood round drinking it awkwardly, the steam rising before their faces, two avoiding each other's eyes, the third staring blindly at the opposite wall. Paul warmed his hands on the cup.

Demelza said: "You can hear the roar upstairs. I thought it was no use."

"It were roarin' last night," Mark said suddenly, "when I come up from the mine. God forgive me, twas roarin' then. . . ."

There was a grim silence.

"You'll stay here to-day?" said Demelza.

Ross said: "I have already asked him but he'll not hear of it."

Demelza glanced at Mark and said no more. He was not to be argued with.

Mark lowered his cup. "I was reckoning to go down Grambler."

There was another silence. Demelza shivered.

Paul hunched his shoulders uncomfortably. "The air may be foul. You know what Grambler always was for foul air. There's easier berths than that."

"I was reckoning," said Mark, "to go down Grambler."

Ross glanced at the sky. "You'll not be there before it is light."

Demelza too glanced out of the window, at the ruin on the sky line. "What of Wheal Grace? Is there still a ladder for that?"

Ross glanced at Mark. "The ladder was sound enough six years ago. You could use a rope to be sure."

Mark said: "I was reckoning to go down Grambler."

"Oh, nonsense, man. No one could blame me for your hiding in Grace. Don't you agree, Paul?"

" 'S I reckon he'd be safe there. What do ee say, old dear? The light's growing fast. No military man would follow down there."

Mark said: "I don't like it. Tes too close to this 'ouse. Folk might suspect."

"I'll go and get you some food," Demelza said.

An hour later the day broke. It was an unhappy day for Demelza, and she had lost her good spirits.

At nine o'clock the burly Sam Jenkins mounted a pony outside his forge and rode over to Mingoose, stopping in to see Dr. Enys on the way. At fifteen minutes to ten Sir Hugh Bodrugan also arrived at Mingoose; the Rev. Mr. Faber, rector of St. Minver Church, followed. The conference lasted until eleven, then a messenger was sent to fetch Dr. Enys. At noon the meeting broke up, Sir Hugh Bodrugan riding over to Trenwith to see Mr. Francis Poldark and then going on to St. Ann's, where he met Mr. Trencrom, and they went together to see the captain of the dragoons. It was a somewhat stormy meeting, for the captain was no fool, and Sir Hugh rode home to dinner with the fine rain to cool his heated whiskery face. Thereafter some hours went by in expectant calm. At four Ross walked down to look at the sea. The gentle rain had quieted it, but there was still an ugly swell. Both low tides would be in daylight, but any time after midnight might do on the falling tide. At five word came through that the soldiers, instead of being set to the man hunt, had been searching the St. Ann's houses all afternoon and had uncovered a fine store of contraband. Ross laughed.

At six three dragoons and a civilian rode down the narrow track of Nampara Combe. Nothing like it had ever been seen before.

Demelza was the first in the house to sight them and she flew into the parlour, where Ross was sitting thinking over his quarrel with Francis.

He said: "No doubt they are making a social call."

"But why come here, Ross, why come here? D'you think someone has told on us?"

He smiled. "Go change your dress, my dear, and prepare to be the lady."

She fled out, seeing through the half-open front door that the civilian was Constable Jenkins. Upstairs she hurriedly changed, to the sound of clopping hooves and the distant rattle of accoutrements. She heard them knock and be shown in;

then the faint murmur of voices. Anxiously she waited, knowing how gentle Ross could be or how much the opposite. But there was no uproar.

She turned her hair here and there with a comb and patted it into place. Then she peeped behind the curtain of the window, to see that only one of the soldiers had entered. The other two, in all the splendour of black and white busbies and red coats, waited with the horses.

As she went down and reached the door there was a sudden tremendous burst of laughter. Heartened, she went in.

"Oh, my dear, this is Captain McNeil of the Scots Greys. This is my wife."

Captain McNeil looked enormous in his red and gold coat, dark gold-braided trousers and spurred shiny boots. On the table stood a huge busby and beside it a pair of yellow gauntlet gloves. He was a youngish man, plump, well groomed, with a great sandy moustache. He set down the glass he was holding and bowed over her hand military fashion. As he straightened up his keen brown eyes seemed to say: "These outlandish country squires do themselves well with their womenfolk."

"You know Constable Jenkins, I think."

They waited until Demelza had taken a chair and then sat down again.

"Captain McNeil has been describing the amenities of our inns," said Ross. "He thinks the Cornish bugs have the liveliest appetite."

The soldier gave a softer echo of his tremendous laugh.

"Nay, I wouldn't say so much as that. Perhaps it is only that there are more of 'em."

"I have offered that he should come and stay with us," said Ross. "We are not rich in comfort but neither are we rich in crawlers." (Demelza blushed slightly at Ross's use of her old word.)

"Thank ye. Thank ye kindly." Captain McNeil twisted one end of his moustache as if it were a screw that must be fastened to his face. "And for old times' sake I should be uncommon pleased to do so. It terrns out, mistress, that Captain Poldark and I were both in a summary affray on the James River in 'eighty-one. Old campaigners together as ye might say.

But though here I would be near the scene of the merrder, I'm much too far from the contraband we picked up this noon, and contraband was what I was sent into this part to find, ye see." He chuckled.

"Indeed," said Demelza. (She wondered what it would feel like to be kissed by a man with a moustache like that.)

"Hrr — hmm," said Constable Jenkins diffidently. "About this murder . . ."

"Och, yes. We mustn't forget——"

"Let me fill your glass," Ross said.

"Thank ye. . . . As I was explaining to your husband, mistress, this is but a routine inquiry, as I understand he was one of the airly finders of the body. Also it is said the wanted man has been seen in this immediate neighbourhood. . . ."

"Really," said Demelza. "I had not heard it."

"Well, so the constable says."

"It was rumoured so, ma'am," Jenkins said hastily. "We don't know where it come from."

"So I made this call to see if ye could advise me. Captain Poldark has known the man since boyhood and I thought perhaps he would have some notion of where he might be lairking."

"You might search for a year," said Ross, "and not exhaust all the rabbit holes. All the same I do not imagine Daniel will linger. I think he will make for Plymouth and join the Navy."

Captain McNeil was watching him. "Is he a good sailor?"

"I have no idea. Every man here has some of the sea in his blood."

"Now tell me, Captain Poldark: are there overmany places on this coast where a boat may be launched?"

"What, a naval boat?"

"No, no, just a small boat which would be handled by one or two men."

"In a flat sea there are half a hundred. In a steep sea there isn't one between Padstow and St. Ann's."

"And what would ye call the present?"

"To-day it is moderate, dropping a little, I fancy. It may be feasible to launch a boat from Sawle by to-morrow evening. Why do you ask?"

Captain NcNeil screwed up his moustache. "Are there overmany suitable boats about whereby a man could make his escape, d'you imagine?"

"Oh, I see your point. No, not that one man could handle."

"Do ye know anyone with a suitable boat at all?"

"There are a few. I have one myself. It is kept in a cave in Nampara Cove."

"Where d'you keep the oars, sur?" ventured Constable Jenkins.

Ross got up. "Can I pursuade you to stay to supper, gentlemen? I will give the order now."

The blacksmith was a little nervous at this favour, but Captain McNeil rose and declined. "One day I'll call again and we'll have a lively crack over old times. But I should appreciate the favour of being shown the cove and cliffs if ye can spare the time now. I have a notion that it would help me one way or another. If ye can shoot at two birds with the one ball as ye might say . . ."

"Well, there is no hurry," said Ross. "Try this brandy first. I trust you will be able to tell from the flavour whether or not duty has been paid on it."

The soldier broke into his great good-humoured laugh.

They chatted a while longer and then the captain took his leave of Demelza. He clicked his heels and bowed low over her hand, so that the soft whiskers of his moustache tickled her fingers. For a second he looked at her with bold admiration in his brown eyes. Then he picked up his gloves and his great busby and clanked out.

When Ross came back from showing him the cove and cliffs Demelza said:

"Phew, I'm that glad it turned out that way. And you were so good. No one would have dreamed you knew anything. What a nice man. I should not mind so much being arrested by him."

"Don't underrate him," Ross said. "He's a Scotsman."

CHAPTER VIII

Heavy windless rain set in as night fell.

At ten, when the tide was nearly full, Ross went down to the cove and saw that the swell had dropped. There could not have been a more favourable night; the darkness was like extra eyelids squeezing away the thought of sight.

At midnight two men waited inside the roofless engine house of Wheal Grace. Paul Daniel, with an old felt hat, and a sack over his shoulder, Ross in a long black cloak that came to his ankles and made him look like a bat. Presently in the depths of the pit there flickered a light.

With the ceaseless drum of the rain in their ears, falling on their hats and bodies and on the long wet grass, they waited and watched.

As he neared the top the light went out.

His head and shoulders showed above the rim of the shaft and he clambered out and sat a moment on his haunches. The rain drummed on the grass.

"I thought twas near morning," he said. "What of the tide?"

"It will do."

They set off down the valley to the house.

"There's money in that mine," said Mark. "To keep from going off my head — I went all over."

"Someday perhaps," said Ross.

"Copper . . . I've never seen a more keenly lode. An' silver lead."

"Where?"

"On the east face. Twill be underwater most times. . . ."

The parlour light showed brightly, but Ross made a detour and came up against the library wall. Then he groped for the door and they were inside in the darkness. There was some scraping and then a candle burned in the far corner — in the corner where Keren had acted and danced.

A meal was set on a table.

Mark said: "Tes dangering you needless." But he ate rapidly while the other two kept watch.

With the lighted parlour as a decoy, Demelza was sitting in the darkness of the bedroom above keeping watch up the valley. After the visit of the soldier Ross was taking no chances.

Very soon Mark was done. He looked terrible to-night, for his strong beard was half an inch long and the heavy rain had washed streaks down the dirt of his face.

"There's this," said Ross, putting forward a parcel of food, "and this." An old coat. "It is the best we can do. You will need all your efforts to be out of sight of the land by morning, for there's no breeze to help you."

Mark said: "If thanks would bring things for ee . . . But listen . . ."

"Tell me on the way down."

"I been thinking of my house, Reath Cottage, that I builded for she. You won't — you won't let it fall down?"

"No, Mark."

"There's stuff in the garden. That's for you, Paul. It has yielded well."

"I'll see for it," said Paul.

"And," said Mark, turning his eyes on Ross, "and there's one thing else. It's . . . You'll see she's buried proper? Not in a pauper's grave. . . . She was above that. . . ."

"I'll see to it," Ross told him.

"There's money under the bed in the cottage. It'll be enough to pay. . . . I'd like a stone. . . ."

"Yes, Mark. We'll see it's done right."

Mark picked up his things, the food, the coat.

"Keren on the stone," he said indistinctly. "She never liked Kerenhappuch. Keren Daniel. Just Keren Daniel. . . ."

They set off for the cove. The rain had not put out the lights of the glowworms. The sea was quieter to-night, grumbling and hissing under the steady downpour. It was not quite so black here, the white fringe of surf was faintly phosphorescent, easing the night's dark weight. They left the stream and moved across the soft sand. They were within a few yards of the cove when Ross stopped. He put out a hand behind and drew Paul level.

"What is that?" he breathed.

Paul put down the mast and stared. He had very sharp eyes, well used to dark places. He bent a little and then straightened.

"A man."

"A soldier," said Ross. "I heard the creak of his belt."

They squatted.

"I'd best go," said Mark.

"Nay, I'll quiet him," said Paul. "They're soft enough under their tall hats."

"No killing," said Ross. "I will do it. . . ." But the elder Daniel had gone.

Ross crouched in the sand, pulling the mast towards him. Mark began to mutter under his breath. He would have given himself up. Ross thought: McNeil has strung his men out all along the cliffs. Shooting at two birds. This way he may either pull in the murderer or some free traders. But if he's watching all points between here and St. Ann's his men will be widely spaced.

Creep forward.

A sudden sharp challenge. They rushed forward. The musket exploded, flat and loud, in the mouth of the cave. A figure sank on to the sand.

"All right," said Paul, short of breath. "But a damnation noise."

"Quick, the boat!"

Into the cave; Ross flung in the mast and the sail; Mark groped for the oars.

"I'll get them; you launch her!"

The brothers began to slide the boat through the soft sand. They had to drag the stirring figure of the soldier aside. Ross came with the oars, thrust them in, put his weight to the boat and it went sliding down towards the sea.

The sound of boots striking rock somewhere, and shouts. Men were coming.

"This way!" shouted a voice. "By the cave!"

Reached the sea. The fringe of surf might show them up.

"Get in!" Ross said through his teeth.

"Rullocks!" said Mark.

Ross took them from his pocket, passed them to Mark; Mark was in: pushed off. A wave broke among them and swung the boat; nearly capsized; back in shallow water. Mark got the oars out.

"Now!"

The noise they were making. Men were running towards them. Shove again together! The boat suddenly came to life, floated off into the blackness. Paul fell on hands and knees in the surf, Ross caught his shoulders, hauled him to his feet. A figure came up and grasped his cloak. Ross knocked the soldier flat on the sand. They ran along the beach. Figures were after them as they turned in towards the stream. Ross changed his course and began to climb up among the bracken that stood four feet high along the side of the combe. They could seek him all night here. Unless they could light a torch they were helpless.

He lay flat on his face for a few minutes gaining his breath, listening to men shouting and searching. Was Paul safe? He moved again. Another danger existed and must be met.

This way it was farther to Nampara. You climbed through the bracken until it gave way to open ground and patches of gorse, then you struck the west corner of the long field and, keeping in the ditch at the side of it, made your way down the hill to the back of the house.

This he did. The Gimletts had been in bed hours, so he slipped in through the kitchen, peeped into the parlour and blew the candles out, quickly mounted the stairs to his bedroom.

Demelza was by the north window but was across the room as soon as his footsteps creaked at the door.

"Are you safe?"

"Ssh! Don't wake Julia." While he told her what had happened he was pulling off his long cloak, dragging his stock from his neck.

"Soldiers! Their . . ."

He sat down suddenly. "Help me, my dear. They may call on us."

She fell on her knees and began to unlace the tall boots in the dark.

"I wonder who gave you away, Ross? *Could* it have been Dwight Enys?"

"Heavens, no! Sound reasoning on the part of the — charming McNeil."

"Oh, Ross, your hands!"

Ross stared closely at them. "I must have cut the knuckles when I hit someone." Then his fingers closed over Demelza's. "You're trembling, love."

"So would you be," she said. "I've been sitting up here alone in the dark, and then those shots . . . ."

Her voice died as a knock came at the front door.

"Now gently, my love, gently. Take your time. That knock is not very peremptory, is it? They are not sure of themselves. We'll wait for another knock before making a light."

He stood up, gathered together the clothes he had taken off and moved to the cupboard.

"No," Demelza said, "under the cot. If you can lift it carefully I'll slip them under."

While they were doing this the knock came again, and louder.

"That should wake Gimlett," said Ross, making a light himself. "He'll think he is always being roused in the middle of the night."

There was water in the room and Demelza hurriedly poured some in a bowl. As the light of the candle grew she took up a flannel and bathed his face and hands. When Gimlett came to the door Ross was just putting on his gown.

"What is it now?"

"If you please, sur, there's a sergeant o' the soldiery askin' to see you downstairs."

"Confound it, this is a time to call! Ask him in the parlour, John. I'll be down very soon."

CHAPTER IX

Mr. Odgers might have thought his pleas effective, for Sawle Feast passed barely marked. But in fact conditions preached the surest sermon.

And the soldiers still lay like a blight on the land. Everyone had been hoping for their going, but instead a contingent moved to Sawle and showed no signs of feeling themselves unwanted. They bivouacked in an open field just behind Dr. Choake's house, and to everyone's disappointment the weather cleared again and no wind blew to strip them in sleep.

Ross had spent an uncomfortable few days. Apart from the chance of trouble over Mark Daniel, there was his breach with Francis. They had never quarrelled in this way before. Even during the ups and downs of these last years Francis and he had always held each other in mutual respect. Ross was not upset at being suspected of helping Verity to elope but at being disbelieved when he denied it. It would never have occurred to him to doubt Francis's word. But it had seemed as if Francis didn't *want* to believe the denial, almost as if he were afraid to believe it. It was all inexplicable and left a nasty taste.

On the Friday, Ross had to go to Trevaunance. Richard Tonkin was to be there, and they were to go into the general accounts before the general meeting that evening. Ever since the opening of the smelting works, opposition to the working of the company had been fierce. Mines had been induced to boycott them, attempts made to squeeze them from the available markets for the refined product; they had been overbid again and again at the ticketings.

But so far they had ridden the storm.

This was the first time Ross had been out since Tuesday evening, and when he reached Grambler he was not overpleased to see a tall cavalry officer coming the other way.

"Why, Captain Poldark." McNeil reined in his horse and bowed slightly. "I was on my way to see ye. Can ye spare the time to turn back for a half-hour?"

"A pleasure I have been looking forward to," Ross said, "but I have a business appointment at Trevaunance. Can you ride with me that far?"

McNeil turned his horse. "Aye, mebbe we can talk a wee bit as we go. I had intended calling on you airlier but I've been more than a little busy what with one thing and another."

"Oh, yes," said Ross, "the smugglers."

"Not only the smugglers. Ye'll remember there was the small matter of that mairderer's escape."

"D'you think he has escaped?"

Captain McNeil screwed his moustache. "Has he not! And from your cove, Captain, and in your boat!"

"Oh, that. I thought it was a brush with the free traders you'd had. The sergeant——"

"I think Sergeant Drummond left ye in no doubt as to his views."

"I judged him mistaken."

"May I ask why?"

"Well, I understand there were several men concerned. Murderers do not hunt in packs."

"No, but he had the sympathy of the neighbourhood."

They jogged along in silence.

"Well, it was a pity you did not catch one of the rascals. Were any of your troopers hurt?"

"Not as ye would say hurrt. Except in a small matter of dignity. It might have gone ill with the lawbreakers if they had been caught."

"Ah," said Ross. And, "Do you know much of churches, Captain? Sawle Church reminds me of one I saw in Connecticut except that it is so badly preserved."

"And then," said the officer, "there was the matter of the rowlocks. How do ye suppose they were got?"

"I should say Daniel — if it was he — stole a pair somewhere. Every man here is a fisherman in his spare time. There are always rowlocks about."

"Ye do not seem very upset at the loss

of your boat, Captain Poldark."

"I am becoming philosophical," Ross said. "As one nears thirty I think it is a state of mind to be sought after. It is a protection, because one becomes more conscious of loss — loss of time, of dignity, of one's first ideals. I'm not happy to lose a good boat, but sighing will not bring it back any more than yesterday's youth."

"Your attitude does you credit," McNeil said dryly. "Might I, as a man a year or so your senior, offer ye a word of advice?"

"Of course."

"Be careful of the law, Captain. It is a cranky, twisty old thing and you may flout it a half dozen times. But let it once come to grips with ye, and ye will find it as hard to be loose from as a black squid. Mind you, I have a sympathy with your point of view. There's something about army life that makes a man impatient of the Justice and the parish constable; I've felt it so myself; indeed I have. . . ." He gave a brief, sudden chuckle. "But that——" He stopped.

Ross said: "See those children, McNeil. It is the only beech copse round here and they are gathering the leaves and will take them home to be cooked. It is not a very nourishing dish and makes their stomachs swell."

"Yes," said the captain grimly. "I see them well."

"I confess I sometimes feel impatient of a lot of things," Ross said. "Including the parish constable and the local magistrates. But I think it dates from earlier in my life than you imagine. I joined the Fifty-second Foot to escape them."

"That's as may be. Once a rebel, always a rebel, you may say. But there are degrees of rebellion, Captain, just as there are degrees of misdemeanour, and when the parish constable comes to be supported by a troop of His Majesty's cavalry——"

"And a crack regiment at that."

"And a crack regiment, as ye say; then recklessness becomes folly and is likely to lead to bad consequences. A military man out of uniform may be no respecter of persons. A military man in uniform will be still less so."

They left Sawle Church behind and took the track past Trenwith.

Ross said: "I feel we have a good deal in common, Captain McNeil."

"That's one way of putting it."

"Well, I have been in and out of scrapes a good part of my life, and I imagine you have been the same."

The captain laughed, and a flock of birds rose from a neighbouring field.

"I think perhaps you will agree," Ross said, "that though we may revere the law in abstract, in practice there are considerations which take a higher place."

"Such as?"

"Friendship."

They rode on in silence.

"The law would not admit that."

"Oh, I do not expect the law to admit it. I was asking you to admit it."

The Scotsman screwed in his moustache. "No, no, Captain Poldark. Oh, dear, no. You are out of uniform but I'm still in it. I'll not be manoeuvred into a corner by such moral arguments."

"But moral argument is the most potent force in the world, Captain. It was that more than force of arms which defeated us in America."

"Well, next time you must try it on my troopers. They will appreciate the change." McNeil reined in his horse. "I think we have gone far enough, Captain."

"It is another mile to Trevaunance yet."

"But farther I doubt before we reach agreement. It's time we parted. I should have appreciated an assurance that ye had taken good heed of my warning——"

"Oh, I have done that, I do assure you."

"Then there's no more need be said — this time. It may be that we shall meet again — in different circumstances, I should hope."

"I shall look forward to it," Ross said. "If you are ever in these parts again consider my house at your disposal."

"Thank you." McNeil extended his hand.

Ross took off his glove and they shook hands.

"Have ye hurt your hand somewhere?" McNeil said, glancing down at the scarred knuckles.

"Yes," said Ross, "I caught it in a rabbit trap."

They saluted and separated, Ross going on his way, McNeil turning back towards Sawle. As the soldier rode away he twisted his moustache vigorously and now and again a subdued laugh shook his big frame.

The smelting works now straggled up the side of Trevaunance Quay.

A long way off it was possible to see the immense volumes of smoke from the furnaces, and on this still day it hung in the valley shutting out the sun. Here was industry with a vengeance, with great piles of coal and heaps of ashes and an unending stream of mules and men busy about the copper house and the quay.

He dismounted first beside the works to look them over.

Several reverberatory furnaces had been built, some for roasting and some for fusing the ore. The copper was roasted and then melted, whilst at intervals the waste was removed, until after twelve hours it was turned out in a molten state into a trough of water. This sudden cooling brought it to a mass of small grains, which were roasted for another twenty-four hours and again turned out, until eventually the coarse copper was run off into sand moulds to cool. This melting and refining had to take place several times before it reached a proper stage of purity. The whole process averaged a fortnight. Small wonder, Ross thought, that it took three times as much coal to smelt a ton of copper as a ton of tin. And coal at fifty shillings a wey.

Although the place had been open only three months he noticed already how ill and wan many of the men were who worked there. The great heat and the fumes were too much for any but the strongest, and there was a higher sickness rate here than in the mines. A factor he had not foreseen. He had laboured long hours to bring this thing to pass, believing it meant prosperity for the district and perhaps salvation for the mines; but there did not seem much prosperity for the poor devils who worked here.

The fumes were blighting the vegetation in this pretty cove. The bracken was brown a month in advance of its time and the leaves of the trees were twisted and discoloured. Thoughtfully he rode up to Place House, which stood on the other side of the valley.

When he was shown in Sir John Trevaunance was still at breakfast and reading the *Spectator*.

"Ah, Poldark, take a seat. You're early. But then I'm late, what? I do not expect Tonkin for half an hour." He flipped the paper. "This is a confoundedly disturbing business, what?"

"You mean the riots in Paris?" said Ross. "A little extravagant."

Sir John put in a last mouthful of beef. "But for the King to give way to them! Ecod he must be a lily! A round or two of grapeshot is what they wanted. It says the Comte d'Artois and several others have left France. To bolt at the first grumble of thunder!"

"Well, I fancy it should keep the French

occupied with their own affairs," Ross said. "England should take the hint and put her own house in order."

Sir John munched and read in silence for a while. Then he crumpled up the paper and threw it impatiently to the floor. The great boarhound by the fireplace rose and sniffed at the paper and then walked off, disliking the smell.

"That man Fox!" said the baronet. "Damme, he's a fool if ever there was one! Going out of his way to praise a rabble such as that. One would think the gates of Heaven had opened!"

Ross got up and walked over to the window. Trevaunance stared after him.

"Come, man, don't tell me you're a Whig! Your family never was, not any of 'em."

"I'm neither Whig nor Tory," Ross said.

"Well, drot it, you must be something. Who d'you vote for?"

Ross was silent again for some time and bent and patted the hound. He seldom thought these things out.

"I'm not a Whig," he said, "nor ever

could belong to a party that was for ever running down its own country and praising up the virtues of some other. The very thought of it sticks in my crop."

"Hear, hear!" said Sir John, picking his teeth.

"But neither could I belong to a party which looks with complacency on the state of England as it is. So you'll see the difficulty I'm in."

"Oh, I don't think——"

"And you must not forget," Ross said, "that it is but a few months since I stormed a gaol of my own. And one which held considerably more than the six prisoners of the Bastille. It is true I didn't parade the streets of Launceston with the gaoler's head stuck on a pole, but that was not for lack of feeling like it."

"Hm!" said Sir John uncomfortably. "Hrrrm! Well, if you will excuse me, Poldark, I'll change my gown to be ready for Tonkin."

He left the room hastily and Ross continued to pat the head of the boarhound.

CHAPTER X

Demelza had been wrestling with her conscience ever since Monday evening, and when Ross left on the Friday she knew she would have no peace unless she gave way.

So after he had gone she walked over to Trenwith. She was almost as nervous as she had ever been in her life, but there was no escape. She had hoped for a letter from Verity yesterday with the *Mercury,* but none had come.

Making the mistake of most early risers, she was surprised to find that Trenwith House had an unawakened look, and when she plucked at the doorbell Mary Bartle told her that Mrs. Poldark was still in bed and that Mr. Poldark was breakfasting alone in the winter parlour.

This might suit better than she had

hoped and she said:

"Could I see him, if you please?"

"I'll go and ask, ma'am, if you'll wait here."

Demelza wandered round the splendid hall, staring up at the pictures, able to take a longer view of them than she had ever done before. A strange crew, more than half of them Trenwiths, Ross said. She fancied she could detect the Poldark strain coming in, the stronger facial bones, the blue, heavy-lidded eyes, the wide mouth. Those early Trenwiths were the men with the looks, soft curling dark beards and sensitive faces, and the red-haired girl in a velvet gown of the style of William and Mary — but perhaps the Poldarks had given a new vigour. Was it they too who had brought the wild strain? Elizabeth had not been painted yet. That was a pity, in fairness Demelza had to admit it.

The house was very quiet, seemed to lack something. She suddenly realized that what it was lacking was Verity. She stood quite still and saw for the first time that she had robbed this household of its most vital personality. She had been the instrument of a theft, perpetrated on Francis and Elizabeth.

She had never looked on it that way before. All the time she had seen Verity's life as incomplete. She had looked at it from Andrew Blamey's point of view but not from Elizabeth's or Francis's. If she had thought of them at all she had considered them as clinging to Verity from selfish motives, because she was so useful to them. It hadn't occurred to her that everyone in this household might in fact love Verity and feel her personal loss — not until she stood in this hall, which seemed so large and so empty to-day. She wondered how she had had the impertinence to come.

"Mr. Poldark will see ee right away," said Mary Bartle behind her.

So while Sir John Trevaunance was entertaining Ross at his breakfast table, Francis was entertaining Demelza.

He got up when she went in. Unlike Sir John he was fully dressed, in a buff-coloured morning coat with velvet lapels, a silk shirt and brown breeches. His look was not friendly.

"I'm sorry," he said shortly, "Elizabeth is not down. She breakfasts upstairs these days."

"I didn't come to see Elizabeth," Demelza answered, flushing. "I came to see you."

"Oh. In that case, please sit down."

"I don't want for you to interrupt your meal."

"It is finished."

"Oh." She sat down, but he stood, a hand on the back of his chair.

"Well?"

"I have come to you to tell you something," she said. "I b'lieve you had a quarrel with Ross over Verity leaving the way she did. You thought he was at fault."

"Has he sent you here this morning?"

"No, Francis; you know he would not do that. But I — I have to clear this up, even if you hate me for it ever after. Ross had nothing to do with Verity's elopement. I know that for certain."

Francis's angry eyes met hers. "Why should I believe you when I have disbelieved him?"

"Because I can tell you who did help."

He laughed shortly. "I wonder."

"Yes, I can. For I was the one who helped, Francis, not Ross. He knew nothing about it. He didn't approve of her going any more than you did."

Francis stared at her, frowned at her, turned sharply away as if shaking her confession aside, went to the window.

"I believed it was . . . I believe it was for Verity's happiness," she stumbled on. She had intended to tell him the whole truth but her courage failed her. "After the Assembly I offered to act as — as a go-between. Captain Blamey wrote to me an' I passed the letters to Verity. She gave letters to me and I gave them to the *Mercury* man. Ross didn't know nothing at all about it."

There was silence. A clock in the room was ticking. Francis took a deep breath, then blew it out slowly on the window.

"You damned interfering . . ." He stopped.

She got up.

"Tisn't pleasant to come here and confess this. I know how you feel for me now. But I couldn't let this quarrel betwixt you and Ross go on from my fault. I didn't wish to hurt you or Elizabeth, please know that. You're right. I was interfering; but if I did wrong twas out of love for Verity, not to hurt you——"

"Get out!" he said.

She began to feel sick. She had not thought the interview would be nearly as bad as this. She had tried to repair a mistake, but it did not seem that she had done any good at all. Was his feeling for Ross any different?

"What I came for," she said, "was to take the blame. If you hate me, that's maybe what I deserve, but please don't let this be a quarrel between you and Ross. I should feel——"

He put up his hand to the catch of the window as if to open it. She saw that his hand was trembling. What was the matter with him?

"Will you go," he said, "and never enter this house again. Understand, so — so long as I live I never want you to come near Trenwith again. And Ross can stay out as well. If he will marry an ignorant trull such as you then he must take the consequences.''

He had controlled his voice so hard that she could only just hear what he said. She turned and left him, went out into the hall, picked up her cloak, passed through the open doorway into the sun. There was a seat beside the wall of the house and she sat on it. She felt faint, and the ground was unsteady.

After a few minutes the breeze began to revive her. She got up and began to walk back to Nampara.

Lord Devoran was not present, being kept away by an attack of tissick. Mr. Trencrom was away also, being still privily occupied with the claims of his suffering employees — those who had had the misfortune to be found with contraband goods in their cellars and lofts.

From the beginning Ross felt there was something wrong. This was a general meeting of the shareholders and as such was not held until after dark. No general meeting had ever yet been held in daylight, since there might always be a spy about watching comings and goings.

A score had turned up. Chief item for discussion was Ray Penvenen's proposal that a rolling and cutting mill should be built at the top of the hill where his land joined Sir John's, he personally to pay half the cost, the company the other half. The project was urgent, for the venturers of Wheal Radiant had suddenly refused to renew the lease on their battery mill. Unless the company put up its own mill at once it would be forced to sell the copper solely in block ingots.

The only debatable point was the selection of site. Nevertheless Ross was for making the concession to Penvenen's *amour-propre,* for Penvenen had what was at a premium, free money. What Ross expected was opposition from Alfred Barbary. And he got it. The dreary old argument was dragged up about the north-coast shareholders' getting all the plums.

Ross listened to the wrangle but noted again that the cross-eyed Aukett sat silent, plucking at his bottom lip. A carpet manufacturer called Fox might have been turned to stone. Presently Tonkin, who made the perfect chairman, said: "I should like the opinion of some of the other shareholders."

After the usual sort of hesitation some views were given, mainly in favour of the mill near the works. Then Aukett said: "It's all very well, gentlemen, but where's our half of the money coming from, eh; that's what I'd like to know?"

Tonkin said: "Well, it was understood by the leading shareholders that additional calls might be expected and we all accepted that. The need is great. If we can't roll and beat the copper we miss nearly all our small markets. And the small markets may just turn the scale. We can't force the Government to buy our copper for the Mint, but we can expect our own friends to buy their requirements from us."

There was a murmur of agreement.

"Well, that's very well," said Aukett, squinting worse than usual in his excitement, "but I'm afraid our mine will be unable to meet any such call. Indeed, it looks as if someone will have to take over the shares I hold."

Tonkin looked at him sharply. "Whether you sell the shares is your own concern, but so long as you retain them you're in honour bound to accept the responsibilities we all jointly incurred."

"And so we'd like to," said Aukett. "But you can't get blood out of a stone. Whether we like it or not we shall have to contract out of the undertaking."

"You mean default?'

"No, there's no question of defaulting. The shares are paid up. And our good will you'll retain, but——"

"What's wrong?" said Blewett. "You told me on Tuesday that the higher prices at the last ticketing had put the Wheal Mexico venturers in better heart than they'd been for years."

"Yes," Aukett nodded. "But yesterday I had a letter from Warleggan's Bank telling me they could no longer support our loan and would we make arrangements to get it transferred elsewhere. That means——"

"You had that?" said Fox.

"That means ruin unless Pascoe's will

take it over, and I have my doubts, for Pascoe's were always on the cautious side and want more security. I'm calling in at Warleggan's on my way home to see if I can persuade them to reconsider it. It's unheard of suddenly to withdraw one's credit like this——"

"Did they give any reason?" Ross asked.

"I had a very similar letter," Fox interrupted. "As you know I have been extending my business in several directions and I have drawn heavily during the last year. I went to see Mr. Nicholas Warleggan last evening and explained that a withdrawal of their facilities would mean the failure of these schemes. He was not very amenable. I believe he knew all about my interest in Carnmore and resented it. I really believe that was at the bottom of it."

"It was." Everyone looked at St. Aubyn Tresize. "My private business is not for discussion at this table, gentlemen. But money has been advanced to me during the last few years from Warleggan's Bank. They have the finest security in the world: land; but it is a security I don't propose to forfeit. If they foreclose at this stage I shall fight them — and they'll not get the land. But they will get most of my assets — including my shares in the Carnmore Copper Company."

"How the Devil have they come to know all this?" Blewett demanded nervously. "More than half of us here have some indebtedness that can be assailed."

"Someone has been talking," said a voice at the bottom.

Richard Tonkin tapped the table. "Has anyone else here had word from the Warleggans?"

There was silence.

"Not yet," said Johnson.

"Well, drot it," said Trevaunance. "You should all bank with Pascoe, as I do; then you'd not get into this mess. Get Pascoe's to take over your accounts."

"Easier said than done," Fox snapped. "Aukett's right. Pascoe's want a better security. I was with them and could not get enough free money and I changed to Warleggan's. So there's small hope of me being able to change back."

Ray Penvenen grunted impatiently. "Well, that's a matter personal to you. We can't all start confessing our private difficulties or it will smack of a Methody revival. Let's get back to this question of the mill."

At length it was agreed that the mill should be put up as a separate venture by Penvenen on the site of his own choosing. The Carnmore Company should hold only thirty per cent of the shares. Unreality had come to sit among them. Very well for Penvenen with his upcountry interests, to dismiss the matter as of no moment. Mines worked on credit, and these were not times for facing its withdrawal. Ross saw the same look on many faces. Someone has let us down. And if three names are known, why not all?

The meeting closed early. Decisions were taken, proposals went through; the name of Warleggan was no more spoken. Ross wondered how many of the decisions would be put into effect. He wondered if there was any danger of their stiff fight becoming a debacle.

When it was over he shook hands all

round and was one of the first to leave. He wanted to think. He wanted to consider where the leak might have occurred. It was not until he was riding home that a very uncomfortable and disturbing thought came to him.

CHAPTER XI

Demelza was in bed but not asleep. When she spoke he gave up the attempt to undress in the dark.

"You're roosting early," he said. "I hope this is a sign of a reformed life."

Her eyes glittered unnaturally in the growing yellow light of the candle.

"Have you any news of Mark?"

"No; it's early."

"There are all sorts of rumours about France."

"Yes, I know."

"How did your meeting go?"

He told her.

She was silent after he had finished. "D'you mean it may make more difficulties for you?"

"It may."

She lay quiet then while he finished

undressing, her hair coiled on the pillow. One tress of it lay on his pillow as he came to get into bed. He picked it up and squeezed it in his fingers a moment before putting it with the rest.

"Don't put out the light," she said. "I've something to tell you."

"Can't you talk in the dark?"

"Not this. The darkness is so heavy sometimes. . . . Ross, I b'lieve we should sleep sweeter without the bed hangings these warm nights."

"As you please." He put the candle beside the bed where it flung yellow fancies on the curtains at their feet.

"Have you heard anything more of Verity?" she asked.

"I've not stirred from Trevaunance Cove all day."

"Oh, Ross," she said.

"What is the matter?"

"I . . . I have been to Trenwith to-day to see Francis."

"The Devil you have! You'd get no welcome there. And certainly no news of Verity."

"It wasn't for news of Verity I went. I

went to tell him he was mistaken in thinking you'd encouraged Verity to elope."

"What good would that do?"

"I didn't want that blame laid to me, that I'd caused a quarrel between you. I told him the truth: that I'd helped Verity unbeknown to you."

She lay very still and waited.

Annoyance was somewhere within him but it would not come to a head: it ran away again into channels of fatigue.

"Oh, Heavens," he said at length, wearily. "What does it matter?"

She did not move or speak. The news sank farther into his understanding, set off fresh conduits of thought and feeling.

"What did he say?"

"He — he turned me out. He — he told me to get out and . . . He was so angry. I never thought . . ."

Ross said: "If he vents his ill-humour on you again . . . I could not understand his attitude to me on Monday. It seemed just as wild and unreasonable as you say——"

"No, Ross, no, Ross," she whispered urgently. "That's not right. It isn't him

673

you should be angry with, it is me. I am in the fault. Even then I didn't tell him all."

"What did you tell him?"

"I — that I had passed on letters from Andrew Blamey and sent him letters from Verity ever since the Assembly in April."

"And what didn't you tell him?"

There was silence.

She said: "I think you will hit me, Ross."

"Indeed."

"I did as I did because I loved Verity and hated her to be unhappy."

"Well?"

She told him everything. Her secret visit to Falmouth while he was away; how she had contrived a meeting and how it had all happened.

He did not interrupt her once. She went right through to the end, faltering but determined. He listened with a curious sense of incredulity. And all the time that other suspicion was beating away. This thing was a part of it: Francis must have realized that Verity and Blamey had been deliberately brought together. Francis had suspected *him*. Francis knew all about the Carnmore Copper Company. . . .

The candle flame shivered and the light broke its pattern on the bed.

It all came round to Demelza. The thing welled up in him.

"I can't believe you did it," he said at last. "If — if anyone had told me I should have named him a liar. I'd *never* have believed it. I thought you were trustworthy and loyal."

She did not say anything.

The anger came easily now; it could not be stemmed.

"To go behind my back. *That* is what I can't stomach or — or even quite believe yet. The deceit——"

"I tried to do it openly. But you wouldn't let me."

She had betrayed him and was the cause of the greater betrayal. It all fitted into place.

"So you did it underhand, eh? Nothing mattered, no loyalty or trust, so long as you got your own way."

"It wasn't for myself. It was for Verity."

"The deceit and the lies," he said with tremendous contempt. "The continual lying for more than twelve months. We have been married no long time but I prided myself that this, this association of ours, was the one constant in my life. The one thing that would be changeless and untouchable. I should have staked my life on it. Demelza was true to the grain. There wasn't a flaw in her—— In this damned world——"

"Oh, Ross," she said with a sudden great sob, "you'll break my heart."

"You expect me to hit you?" he said. "That's what you can understand. A good beating and then over. But you're not a dog or a horse to be thrashed into the right ways. You're a woman, with subtler instincts of right and wrong. Loyalty is not a thing to be bought: it is freely given or withheld. Well, by God, you have chosen to withhold it . . . !"

She began to climb out of bed, blindly; was out and clung sobbing to the curtains, released them and groped round the bed. Her whole body shook as she wept.

As she reached the door he sat up. His

anger would not subside.

"Demelza, come here!"

She had gone and had shut the door behind her.

He got out of bed, took up the candle and opened the door again. She was not on the stairs. He went down shedding grease, reached the parlour. She was trying to close the door but he flung it open with a crash.

She fled from him towards the farther door, but he put down the candle and caught her by the fireplace and pulled her back. She struggled in his arms, feebly, as if grief had taken her strength. He caught her hair and pulled her head back. She shook it.

"Let me go, Ross. Let me go."

He held her while the tears ran down her cheeks. Then he let her hair go and she stood quiet, crying against him.

She deserves all this and more, he thought. More, more! Let her suffer! He could well have struck her, taken a belt to her. Drunken hind and common drudge. What a foul mixture and mess!

Damn her for an impudent brat! Verity

married to Blamey and all, *all* this trouble through her meddling. He could have shaken her till her teeth chattered.

But already his sense of fairness was fighting to gain a word. It was her fault in part, but not her blame. At least not the consequences. Verity married to Blamey might be the least of them. Damn Francis. Incredible betrayal! (Did he run too fast and too far? No, for it surely all fitted.)

"Come, you'll get cold," he said roughly.

She took no notice.

She had already had the quarrel with Francis. That too must have upset her, for she had been very low when he got home. Curious that that should have upset her so much.

His anger was slowly subsiding, not disappearing but finding its true level. She could not stand his tongue. What had he said? Or *how* had he said it? The Poldarks were an unpleasant lot when they were crossed. Damn Francis, for all this trouble really lay at his door: the first break between Verity and Blamey, his later obstinate refusal to reconsider his dislike! Demelza no doubt had acted for the best. The road to Hell being so paved.

But she had no *right* to act so, for best or worst. She had no *right*. She had interfered and lied to him; and although now she was desperately upset, in a day or two she would be happy and smiling again. And all the consequences would go on and on and on, echoing in this man's life and that.

She had stopped now and she broke away from him.

"I'll be all right," she said.

"Well, do not stay down here all night."

"You go on. I'll come in a little."

He left her the candle and went back to the bedroom. He lit another candle and walked over to the cot. Julia had kicked off all the bedclothes. She was lying like a Muslim worshipper, her head down and her seat in the air. He was about to cover her when Demelza came in.

"Look," he said.

She came over and gave a little gulping "Oh," when she saw the child. She swallowed and turned her over. Julia's curly brown hair was like a halo for the innocent cherubic face. Demelza went quietly away.

Ross stayed staring down at the child, and when he returned Demelza was already in bed. She was sitting well back among the curtains, and he could only see the pyramid of her knees.

Presently he got in beside her and blew out the candle and lay down. She did not move to settle for a long time. Extravagant and contrary in all things, he thought: her loyalties, her griefs. She betrays me, deceives me without a flicker out of love for Verity. Am I to blame her, who know so much about conflicting and divided loyalties?

She causes this breach between Francis and me. The enormity of it, bringing perhaps failure and ruin.

"Ross," she said suddenly, "is it as bad as all that, what I've done?"

"No more talk now."

"No, but I must know that. It didn't seem so wrong to me at the time. I knew it was deceiving you, but I thought I was doing what was best for Verity. Truly I did. Maybe it's because I don't know any better, but that's what I thought."

"I know you did," he said. "But it isn't just that. Other things have come into it."

"What other things?"

"Nothing I can tell you yet."

"I'm that sorry," she said. "I never dreamed to make trouble between you and Francis. I never *dreamed*, Ross. I'd never ha' done it if I thought that."

He sighed. "You have married into a peculiar family. You must never expect the Poldarks to behave in the most rational manner. I have long since given up expecting it. We are hasty — quite incredibly hasty, it seems — and sharp-tempered; strong in our likes and dislikes and unreasonable in them — more unreasonable than I ever guessed. Perhaps, so far as the first goes, yours is the common-sense view. If two people are fond of each other let 'em marry and work out their own salvation, ignoring the past and damning the consequences. . . ."

There was another long silence.

"But I — I still don't understand," she said. "You seem to be talking in riddles,

Ross. An' I feel such a cheat and — and so horrible. . . ."

"I can't explain more now. It is impossible until I am sure. But as for what I said . . . I spoke in heat. So forget it if you can and go to sleep."

She slid an inch farther down the bed.

She blew out a long breath. "I wish — I shall not be very happy if this quarrel between you and Francis does not quickly heal."

"Then I am afraid you will be unhappy for a long time."

Silence fell and this time was not broken. But neither of them went to sleep. She was on edge after the quarrel, desperately unsatisfied and not much relieved by her tears. She felt insecure and much in the dark. She had been told of other reasons for his anger but could not guess them. She bitterly hated anything to be incomplete, especially to leave a trouble unresolved. Yet she knew she could go no further to-night. He was restless and overtired and uneasy. Thoughts ran through his head in endless procession. After a time she closed her eyes and tried to go to sleep. But he did not even try.

BOOK FOUR

CHAPTER I

On Christmas Eve Demelza opened a letter from Verity which ran as follows:

My Dear Cousin Demelza,
  Your welcome letter reached me yesterday morning and I am replying — prompt for me! — to say how pleased I am to learn all are well, with all this sickness abroad. In this Town it is very bad, two or three things rage and who has not got one takes another. However, thanks to God, we too escape, at Church on Sundays the Pews were but half filled owing to it, and afterwards we called on Mrs. Daubuz the mayor's wife to condole with her on the loss of her baby son. We found her very sad but resigned, she is a fine woman.

I am glad that you have at last had news that Mark Daniel is safe in France — that is if anyone can be safe there at this present. It was a horrible thing to happen and I wish it had never been, I can sympathize with Mark but not condone his act.

We have been very busy here for a week past. The East India Fleet consisting of three fine ships and a frigate, with two Fleets from the West Indies as well as one from Oporto bound home are all come into our port except a few from the Leeward Islands, which are gone up Channel. The Harbour is a fine sight with above 200 sail of Vessels in view from our House. The Fleets are very valuable and the Town is full of Passengers from them.

Well my dear I am very happy in my new life. I think age is much how you feel, as a spinster of nearly thirty-one I felt old and sere but as a married woman I do not at all seem the same. I have put on weight since I came and get no more Catarr, perhaps it is the softer Climate which suits me, but I think that is not it. Andrew too is happy and is always whistling in the house. It is strange because no one at Trenwith ever whistled. Some things I miss terrible, some of my old work, and often I long to see the old faces, especially when Andrew is away, but so far my dear you can claim that your faith in us has not gone Awry. Bless you for all you did.

I could have wished that this Christmas time could have seen a reconsiling of us all, a real gathering of just the six of us, with of course Julia and Geoffrey Charles. That would have been good, alas I'm afraid Francis will never soften. But I know Ross will, and in the Spring when the weather improves and Ross is less busy I want you both to come over and spend a week with me. We have quite a number of friends and no one dislikes Andrew who knows him well.

My dear I am so sorry that all Ross's work seems to be coming to nought, it is too bad and such a Pity, for the industry needs all the help it can get, there are distressed tinners round here and some entered the Town last week and made a disturbance. So far it has been a terrible winter and I hope and pray with so many near starving that nothing will happen here like what has happened across the water. Try not to let Ross take this to heart as sometimes he is inclined to do, feeling that any failure is *his* failure. If the very worst comes and the smelting works closes it may be only a setback for a few years, and happier times will see a reopening. Captain Millett one of the Frigate Captains said yesterday that what we need is another war. A terrible solution, but there were others in the room to agree with him. Better Poverty than that, I say.

My only regret is that Andrew is away so much. He leaves this evening and will be gone all Christmas and into the New Year. I have thought often to go with him but he says wait until the summer when the Bay of Biscay will not be so Steep. He loves the sea devotedly but is known throughout the Service as a "driver." Always when he comes home he seems strained, as if the voyage has tried his nerves, he is easier to cross and a trifle moody. I think too he drinks a little during his time at sea, no wonder, for he needs something to sustane him, but never touches a drop while ashore. It takes me one day of his precious time at home to make him quite content, then soon he has to be up and away.

I have not met my two "children" yet. That is something of an Ordeal which may be mine about Easter, when *The Thunderer* with James Blamey on board as a cadet, is expected home. Esther Blamey, Andrew's daughter, is at boarding school and lives with his Sister near Plymouth. It may be that she will come and visit us too in the Spring. Pray for me then! I do so wish to make a home for them here and to make them welcome, if only our relationship will allow. I sometimes think I am such a poor mixer and wish I had an Easy manner, which some people have.

Our housekeeper, Mrs. Stevens was taken so ill with pains in the stomach last night that we sent for Dr. Silvey, but he said it was cramp and gave her a piece of roll Brimstone sewed in fine linen to hold near the affected part when she felt the pain. This has been a wonderful cure, but for my part I do not think she takes enough rhubarb.

I shall think of you this Christmas. I am very, very glad you gave me the courage to make my own life.

God bless and keep you both

Verity

CHAPTER II

Ten o'clock had struck before Ross returned that night. It was a fine night and an hour before Sawle Church choir had been up to the door singing carols. Demelza had never had much to do with religion but she still said the prayers her mother taught her, adding a postscript of her own to keep them abreast of the times; and at Christmas she had always felt an inward impulse to go to church. Something in the ancient wisdom of the story and the fey beauty of the carols tugged at her emotions; and with a suitable invitation she would have been willing to join the choir. She specially wanted to help them this evening, hearing their depleted voices struggling through "Remember, O thou Man." But even her enjoyment of the two carols was a little

693

spoiled by anxiety as to how she had best behave when they knocked on the door. She sent Jane Gimlett for the cakes she had made that afternoon and took down a couple of bottles of canary wine from Ross's cupboard.

They came in, a sheepish, blinking, uncertain lot, headed by Uncle Ben Tregeagle; ill-clad and undernourished every one, and only eight in all, for two of the choir were ill with the ulcerous sore throat and three were sick with influenza and Sue Baker had her fits. So Uncle Ben said, looking sly and foreign with his hooked nose and his long greasy black hair curling in little ringlets on his shoulders.

Demelza nervously gave them all a drink and took one herself; she would almost sooner have entertained Sir Hugh Bodrugan than these humble choristers; at least she knew where she was with him. She pressed cakes on them and refilled their glasses and when they rose to go she gave them a handful of silver — about nine shillings in all — and they crowded out into the misty moonlit night, flushed and merry and opulent. There they gathered round the lantern and gave her one more carol for luck before filing off up the valley towards Grambler.

Laughing now at her own absurdity and her success in spite of it, she went back into the parlour and began to pick out on the spinet the simple tune of "In Dulce Jubilo." Then she sat down and filled in with the other hand. She was getting good at this, though Mrs. Kemp frowned on it and said it wasn't music at all.

While she was so playing she heard Ross return. She met him at the door and at once saw how everything was.

"I've saved some pie for you," she said. "Or there's cold chicken if you want. And some nice fresh cakes and tarts."

He sat down in his chair and she helped him off with his boots.

"I had supper with Tonkin. Not a feast but enough to satisfy. A glass of rum will do and a bite or two of your cake. Have we had visitors?"

Demelza explained. "There's a letter here from Verity. It came this morning."

Ross read it slowly, puckering his eyes as if they too were tired. She put her hand on his shoulders, reading it again with him, and he put his fingers over hers.

The quarrel between them on that July evening had long been ignored but never forgotten. It had been ignored, and for that reason was still felt more by her than by him, it being her temperament to dislike anything not clear and downright. Also he had been fighting other things all these months and away more than at home. That he suspected Francis of betrayal had come to her gradually, and with it all the rest of his reasoning; so that she sometimes felt not only responsible for his quarrel with his cousin but also for the mounting difficulties of the copper company. It was not a pleasant thought and had lain heavy on her, far heavier than he knew. It was the first real shadow on their relationship and it had spoiled her happiness all this autumn. But outwardly there was no change.

"So your experiment prospers more than mine," he said. "Perhaps your instinct was the surer."

"Is there no better news for you?"

"Johnson and Tonkin and I have gone

through the books item by item. Sir John has come to the view, which I think will be general among those who are left, that it is better to cut our losses than to refuse to admit defeat. There will be a final meeting after the ticketing on Monday. If the decision goes against us I will spend Tuesday helping to wind up our affairs.''

"Who are for going on, do you know?''

"Tonkin of course, and Blewett and Johnson. All men of good will and no financial standing. Lord Devoran is for going on so long as he is asked for no more money. Penvenen is already considering converting his mill to other uses.''

Demelza sat down beside him. "You'll have till Monday free?''

"Yes — to make merry over Christmas.''

"Ross, don't get bitter. You see what Verity says.''

He sighed, and the sigh turned to a yawn.

". . . She says you feel everything too deep and that is the trouble, I b'lieve. What difference will it make to our money, Ross?''

"I may have to sell some of the Wheal Leisure shares."

"Oh, no!"

"Perhaps only half — those I bought from Choake."

"But they are paying a — a dividend, d'you call it — it would be such a shame! Is Harris Pascoe not a friend of yours?"

"He's a banker, my dear. His first obligation is to his depositors."

"But he must have a pile of money heaped up in the vaults. It would be no use to him! He knows he will be safe with your promise to pay. Why, you will be able to pay him in a few years out of the div — what I said — if he will only give you time."

Ross smiled. "Well, that will all be thrashed out. I shall have to be in Truro for two days, and Pascoe has invited me to stay with him. It will be difficult for him to be too hard on a guest."

Demelza sat in gloomy silence, nursing her knees.

"I don't like it," she said at length. "It isn't fair, Ross! It is wicked an' inhuman. Have bankers got no Christian bowels?

Don't they ever think, 'How should I feel if I was in debt?' "

"Come, my dear; don't you get too despondent or we shall be a pretty pair to wish each other a happy Christmas."

"Ross, could we not raise a mortgage on this house?"

"It's already raised."

"Or sell the horses and the oxen. I don't mind walking about my business or going short of some foodstuffs — it is only what I was always used to. Then there is my best silver frock and my ruby brooch. You said that was worth a hundred pounds."

He shook his head. "All told these things wouldn't discharge the debt, nor half of it. We must accept the position if it has to be."

"*Is* there a chance of going on?"

"Something will depend on the ticketing on Monday. And there is a movement on to drop the smelting but prevent the failure by becoming merchants pure and simple. I dislike facesaving."

Demelza looked at him. She wondered if she was very selfish to feel glad that in the coming year there might be fewer calls on his time. If the failure of the company meant a return to the old ways then there was some recompense even in failure.

Christmas passed quietly inside Nampara and out — the calm before the storm. He had had scarcely so much leisure since the project took shape. They had worked shorthanded on the farm all through the summer to cut down expense. He had scraped to put everything into Carnmore, and now it seemed he might just as well have thrown it over the cliff.

A bitter reflection but one that had to be faced. Ever since that meeting of the company in July, Ross and his fellow shareholders had been fighting a losing battle. St. Aubyn Tresize, Aukett and Fox had all as good as resigned that day, and since then almost every week had seen a fresh casualty. Those the Warleggans could not touch directly they worked round to affect indirectly. Miners found their credit suddenly withdrawn or their coal supplies held up. Sir John was still fighting his case in Swansea. Alfred

Barbary's title to some of the wharves he used in Truro and Falmouth was called in question, and litigation was pending here until he contracted out of the Carnmore. Even Ray Penvenen was not immune.

Of course it was not all the Warleggans, but it was the result of forces put in motion by them. If their grip had been complete the company could not have survived a month, but there were gaps in all their schemes. Only one third of the other copper companies were directly controlled by them, the rest were in friendly co-operation with the same ends in view.

On Boxing Day, the only windy day of the week, Ross and Demelza rode over to Werry House to visit Sir Hugh Bodrugan. Ross disliked the man but he knew Demelza had been secretly hankering to go ever since her first invitation nine months ago and he felt it right to humour her. They found Sir Hugh bottling gin, but he gave up with a good grace and ushered them into the great parlour, where Constance, Lady Bodrugan, was busy among her puppies.

She was not so rude as Ross remembered her, and received them without blasphemy. She had got used to the strange idea of her elderly stepson's having this liking for Ross Poldark's underbred wife. They took tea at a respectful distance from the greatest log fire Demelza had ever seen, and surrounded by spaniels, boarhound puppies and other breeds, whom Constance fed with cakes from the table and who made polite conversation a tenuous affair punctuated by the snaps and snarls of the disputing feeders. Every now and then a great gust of smoke would billow out from the fireplace, but the room was so high that the fog made a canopy over them and drifted away through the cracks in the ceiling. In this peculiar atmosphere Demelza sipped strong tea and tried to hear what Constance was saying about her treatment for dog's distemper; Ross, looking very tall and rather out of place on a chair too small for him, nodded his lean intelligent head and threw the ball of conversation back at Sir Hugh, who was just then leaning back scratching his ruffles and wondering what sort of fun Demelza would really be in bed.

After tea Sir Hugh insisted on showing them the house and the stables, although by then darkness was near. They walked down draughty passages, led and followed by a groom with a horn lantern, up staircases to a great room on the first floor once elaborately decorated but now damp and mildewed, with creaking boards and cracked windows. Here the Dowager Lady kept her yellow rabbits in great boxes along one wall and bred her puppies in boxes opposite. The smell was overpowering. In the next room was a family of owls, some dormice, a sick monkey and a pair of racoons. Downstairs they went again, to a passage full of cages with thrushes, goldfinches, canary birds and Virginia nightingales. Sir Hugh squeezed her arm so often that Demelza began to wonder if this show was all a pretext for being with her in dark and draughty places. In one room, where the wind was so high that they might have been out of doors, the rear lantern went out and Sir Hugh put his short thick arm round her waist. But she slipped away with a faint rustle of silk and moved quickly up to Ross.

The stables were the best-kept part of the house, with many fine hunters and a pack of hounds, but inspection was abandoned halfway, Lady Bodrugan not being concerned for the comfort of her guests but thinking the horses would be needlessly disturbed.

So back they went to the great parlour, in which the fog had thickened since they left. Demelza had not yet learned to play whist, so they had a hand of quadrille for an hour, at which she won five shillings. Then Ross got up and said they must go before the wind grew worse. Sir Hugh, perhaps with vague hopes of further intimacies, suggested they should stay the night, but they thanked him and refused.

On the way home Demelza was silent, more silent than the gusty night dictated. When they got into the shelter of their own combe she said:

"It isn't always the people with the biggest house who are the most comfortable, is it, Ross?"

"Nor the best-bred who are the cleanest!"

She laughed. "I did not fancy staying there the night. The wind was everywhere. And I should have dreamed of finding that old sick monkey in my bed."

"Oh, I don't think Sir Hugh is sick."

Her laughter bubbled up again, overflowed and ran with the wind.

"Serious, though," she said breathlessly, "what is the use of a big house if you cannot keep it nice? Are they short of money?"

"Not desperate. But old Sir Bob squandered most of what was not entailed."

"It must be strange to have a stepson old enough to be your father." Little eddies of laughter still bubbled inside her. "Serious, though, Ross, would he have money to loan you to tide you over just for the present?"

"Thank you, I would rather the company was put away decently."

"Is there no one else? Would old Mr.

Treneglos help? He has done well out of the mine you started for him. How much do you need to carry on a while longer?"

"A minimum of three thousand pounds."

She pursed her lips together as if to whistle. Then she said: "But for yourself, Ross, so as not to have to sell the Wheal Leisure shares. That's what I care about most of all."

"I shall be more sure when I've talked of it with Pascoe," Ross said evasively. "In any event I would not be willing to borrow from friends."

CHAPTER III

He would not be willing to borrow from friends.

He said that to himself as he left for Truro on the Monday morning. At heart he would have agreed with Demelza, that his own happiness lay with her and little Julia and having leisure to labour on his own land and to see it grow. That was what he had thought at the beginning and nothing could alter it. He might even look back on this year as a nightmare well over and best forgotten. Yet nothing would remove the stigma of the failure, nothing would remove the sting of the Warleggan triumph.

And nothing would salve the bitter disappointment of having to part with the whole of his holding in Wheal Leisure, which he knew was coming, though he had hidden it from Demelza. To lose that was the worst blow of all.

At the clump of firs Zacky Martin was waiting.

The pony and the horse fell naturally into step, having now made many journeys together. Ross tried to forget the business on hand and asked after Zacky's family. The Martins were a tenacious stock. Mrs. Zacky made them all drink pilchard oil during the winter and although it was foul and stank it seemed to be to their good. Jinny's three were brave, thanking you, Zacky said; and Jinny herself more better in spirits. There was a miner at Leisure called Scoble, a widow man in the thirties, lived beyond Marasanvose, no doubt Captain Poldark knew him.

"You mean Whitehead?"

"That's of him. They call him that on account of his hair. Well, he's taking an interest in Jinny, and she won't have nothing to do with him. Tisn't as she dislike him, she say, but that no one could do for Jim's place. That's well enough and as it should be, her mother say, but you've three young children to think of, and he's a nice steady feller with a little cottage, still some years to run and no children of his own. Mebbe in a year or so, Jinny say, I could consider it, but not yet for a while, twouldn't be possible. That's well enough, her mother say, but he's lonely and you're lonely, and men don't always wait and wait, for there's other girls'd be glad of the chance and they single and no family.''

Ross said: ''There is a lot in what Mrs. Zacky says. And no need to fear appearances. I know a clergyman in Truro called Halse who married his second wife within two months of losing his first. It is nothing unusual in the upper classes.''

''I'll tell her that. It may help her to see it right. It is no good to marry a man if you dislike him; but I don't think she do; and I b'lieve it would do her good once the ice was broke.''

When they reached the fork near Sawle Church they saw Dwight Enys, and Ross waved a hand and would have branched off towards the Bargus crossroads, but Dwight signalled him to stop. Zacky rode on a few paces to be out of earshot.

As Dwight came up Ross noticed how his good looks had become cadaverous.

His place in the countryside was secure enough now; his work during the epidemics of the autumn had made sure of that. All remembered and a few still whispered behind his back, but none wished him gone. They liked him, they respected his work, they depended on him. Since the closing of Grambler many of Choake's former patients had come to Enys. Not that such work showed much return, but no one ever asked in vain. He was working off the disgrace within himself. But when not working he liked to be alone.

"You look in need of a holiday," Ross said. "I am lying to-night with the Pascoes and they would be pleased to see you."

Dwight shook his head. "It is out of the question, Ross. There is a mountain of work. If I was absent for three days I should never catch up in three months."

"You should leave Choake more to do. It is not a fair distribution, for you do a hundred poor cases and he does ten rich."

Dwight said: "I am getting along. Old Mr. Treneglos called me in last week for his gout, and you know how he distrusts our profession." The smile faded. "But what I had to tell you is not good news. It is about Mr. Francis Poldark. Had you heard? They say he is ill, also their little son."

"Oh . . . ? No. Have you seen them?"

"Dr. Choake is of course in charge. It is rumoured it is the sore throat. *Morbus strangulatorius.*"

Ross stared at him. This disease had been hanging round the district for nearly nine months. It had never been quite epidemic in the way the familiar diseases were epidemic; but it struck here and there with great rapidity and terrible results. Sometimes a whole family of children was swept off. It flared up in this village or that and then went underground again.

"Only last week," Dwight said, frowning, and as if following his thoughts, "I looked up what records there were on the matter. There was a bad outbreak in 'forty-eight. In Cornwall, that was. But since then we have been tolerably immune.''

''What is the cause?''

''No one knows. Some put it down to a mephitic quality of the air, especially when near water. All our views are much in the melting pot since Cavendish proved there was both dephlogisticated and inflammable air.''

''I wish you could get to see them, Dwight.'' Ross was thinking of Elizabeth.

The younger man shook his head. ''Unless I am called in . . . Besides, I lay no claim to a cure. The results are always unpredictable. Sometimes the strong will go and the weak survive. Choake knows as much as I do.''

''Don't belittle yourself.'' Ross hesitated, wondering whether he should obey his impulse to ride at once and see Elizabeth. It was the Christian thing to do, to forget all the old bitterness. Almost impossible with the copper company dying before his eyes. And the ticketing would not wait. He had only just time to get there.

As he was hesitating, Dr. Choake himself topped the hill out of Sawle riding towards them. . . .

"You'll pardon me," Dwight said. "This man has tried to make every sort of trouble for me. I don't wish to meet him now." He took off his hat and moved away.

Ross stood his ground until Choake was fairly up with him. The physician would have ridden by without a word if he could have got past.

"Good day to you, Dr. Choake."

Choake looked at him from under his eye-thatches.

"We'll trouble you to move aside, Mister Poldark. We are on urgent business."

"I'll not detain you. But I hear that my cousin is gravely ill."

"Gravely ill?" Choake bent his eyebrows after the departing figure of his rival. "Dear me, I should not be inclined to lend an ear to every story if I were you."

Ross said curtly: "Is it true that Francis has the malignant sore throat?"

"I isolated the symptoms yesterday. But he is on the mend."

"So soon?"

"The fever was checked in time. I emptied the stomach with fever powder and gave him strong doses of Peruvian bark. It is all a question of competent treatment. You are fully at liberty to inquire at the house." Choake moved to edge his horse past. Darkie blew through her nostrils and stamped.

"And Geoffrey Charles?"

"Not the throat at all. A mild attack of quartan fever. And the other cases in the house are the ulcerous throat, which is quite a different thing. And now good day to you, sir."

When Choake was past Ross sat a moment gazing after him. Then he turned and followed Zacky.

The ticketing was over and the feast about to begin.

Everything had gone according to plan, someone else's plan. The usual care had been taken to see that the Carnmore Copper Company did not get any of the copper. The mines did well out of it — so long as the Carnmore was in existence as a threat. As soon as Zacky ceased to put in his bids the prices would drop into the ruck again.

Ross wondered if the mines — the remaining mines — were really as powerless as the Warleggans had shown them up to be. They had not been able to stay together so they had fallen by the way. It was a dismal, sordid, disheartening business.

Ross sat down at the long dinner table with Zacky on his one hand and Captain Henshawe, representing Wheal Leisure, on his other. It wasn't until he was served that he noticed George Warleggan.

Ross had never seen him before at a ticketing dinner. He had no plain business there, for although he owned the controlling interest in a number of ventures he always acted through an agent or a manager. Strange that he had condescended, for as George grew more powerful he grew more exclusive. A brief silence had fallen on the men gathered there. They knew all about Mr.

Warleggan. They knew he could make or break a good many if he chose. Then George Warleggan looked up and caught Ross's eye. He smiled briefly and raised a well-groomed hand in salute.

It was a sign for the dinner to begin.

Ross had arranged to meet Richard Tonkin at the Seven Stars Tavern before the others arrived. As he came out of the Red Lion Inn he found George Warleggan beside him. He fell into step.

"Well, Ross," he said in a friendly fashion, as if nothing had happened between them, "we see little of you in Truro these days. Margaret Vosper was saying only last night that you had not been to our little gaming parties recently."

"Margaret Vosper?"

"Did you not know? The Cartland has been Margaret Vosper these four months, and already poor Luke is beginning to fade. I do not know what there is fatal about her, but her husbands seem unable to stand the pace. She is climbing the ladder and will marry a title before she's done."

"There is nothing fatal in her," Ross said, "except a greed for life. Greed is always a dangerous thing."

"So she sucks the life out of her lovers, eh? Well, you should know. She told me she'd once had the fancy to marry you. It would have been an interesting experiment, ecod! I imagine she would have found you a hard nut."

Ross glanced at his companion as they crossed the street. They had not met for eight months; and George, Ross thought, was becoming more and more a "figure." In his early days he had striven to hide his peculiarities, tried to become polished and bland and impersonal, aping the conventional aristocrat. Now with success and power firmly held, he was finding a new pleasure in allowing those characteristics their freedom. He had always tried to disguise his bullneck in elaborate neckcloths; now he seemed to accentuate it slightly, walking with his head thrust forwards and carrying a long stick. Once he had raised his naturally deep voice; now he was letting it go, so that the refinements of speech he had learned and clung to seemed to take on a bizarre quality. Everything about his face was big, the heavy nose, the pursed mouth, the wide eyes. Having as much money as he wanted, he lived now for power. He loved to see himself pointed out. He delighted that men should fear him.

"How is your wife?" George asked. "You do not bring her out enough. She was much remarked on at the celebration ball, and has not been seen since."

"We have no time for a social round," Ross said. "And I don't imagine we should be the more wholesome for it."

George refused to be ruffled. "Of course you will be busy. This copper-smelting project takes a good portion of your time." A pretty answer.

"That and Wheal Leisure."

"At Wheal Leisure you are fortunate in the grade of your ore and the easy drainage. One of the few mines which still offer prospects for the investor. I believe some of the shares are shortly coming on the market."

"Indeed. Whose are they?"

"I understood," said George delicately, "that they were your own."

They had just reached the door of the Seven Stars, and Ross stopped and faced the other man. These two had been inimical since their school days but had never come to an outright clash. Seeds of enmity had been sown time and again but never reached fruit. It seemed that the whole weight of years was coming to bear at once.

Then George said in a cool voice but quickly: "Forgive me if I am misinformed. There was some talk of it."

The remark just turned away the edge of the response that was coming. George was not physically afraid of a rough and tumble but he could not afford the loss to his dignity. Besides, when quarrelling with a gentleman it might not end in fisticuffs even in these civilized days.

"You have been misinformed," Ross said, looking at him with his bleak pale eyes.

George humped his shoulders over his stock. "Disappointing; I am always out for a good speculation, you know. If you ever do hear of any coming on the market, let me know. I'll pay thirteen pound fifteen a share for 'em, which is more than you — more than anyone would get at present in the open market." He glanced spitefully up at the taller man.

Ross said: "I have no control over my partners. You had best approach one of them. For my part I would sooner burn the shares."

George stared across the street. "There is only one trouble with the Poldarks," he said after a moment. "They cannot take a beating."

"And only one trouble with the Warleggans," said Ross. "They never know when they are not wanted."

George's colour deepened. "But they can appreciate and remember an insult."

"Well, I trust you will remember this one." Ross turned his back and went down the steps into the tavern.

CHAPTER IV

It was afternoon before Demelza heard
the bad news of Trenwith. All three of the
younger Poldarks had it, said Betty
Prowse, with only Aunt Agatha well, and
three out of the four servants had taken it.
Geoffrey Charles was near to death, they
said, and no one knew which way to turn.
Demelza asked for particulars, but Betty
knew nothing more. Demelza went on
with her baking.

But not for long. She picked up Julia,
who was crawling about on the floor under
her feet and carried her into the parlour.
There she sat on the rug and played with
the child before the fire while she
wrestled with her torment.

She owed them nothing. Francis had
told her never to come near the house
again. Francis had betrayed them to the

Warleggans. A despicable, horrible thing to do.

They would have called in others to help, perhaps some of the Teague family or one of the Tremenheere cousins from farther west. Dr. Choake would have seen to that for them. They were well able to look after themselves.

She threw the linen ball back to Julia who, having rolled on it to stop it, now forgot her mother and began to try to pull the ball apart.

There was no reason for her to call. It would look as if she were trying to curry favour and patch up the quarrel. Why should she patch it up, when Elizabeth was her rival. Elizabeth had not appeared so much in that light this last year; but she was always a danger. Once Ross saw that fair fragile loveliness . . . She was the unknown, the unattainable, the mysterious. His wife he knew would be here always, like a faithful sheep dog, no mystery, no remoteness, they slept in the same bed every night. They gained in intimacy, lost in excitement. Or that was how she felt it must be with him. No;

leave well alone. She had done enough interfering.

"Ah — ah!" Demelza said. "Naughty girl. Don't tear it abroad. Throw it back to Mummy. Go to! Push with your hand. Push!"

But it was her interference which put her in an obligation deep down. If she had not contrived Verity's marriage, Verity would have been there to take charge. And if she had not so contrived Francis would never have quarrelled with Ross or betrayed them. Was it really all her fault? Sometimes she thought Ross thought so. In the night — when she woke up in the night — she felt that sense of guilt. She glanced out of the window. Two hours of daylight. The ticketing would be over. He would not be home to-night, so she could not have his advice. But she did not want his advice. She knew what she knew.

Julia was crowing on the rug as she went to the bell. But she did not pull it. She could never get used to having servants at call.

She went through to the kitchen. "Jane, I am going out for a while. I expect to be back before dark. If not, could you see to put Julia to bed? See the milk be boiled an' see she takes all her food.''

"Yes, ma'am.''

Demelza went upstairs for her hood and cloak.

The company had assembled in the private room of the Seven Stars. They were a depleted and a subdued party. Lord Devoran was in the chair. He was a fat dusty man in snuff brown, and he had a cold in the head from leaving off his wig.

"Well, gentlemen,'' he said stuffily, "you have heard Mr. Johnson's statement of accounts. It is all very disappointing I aver, for the company was started in such high hopes not fourteen months ago. It has cost me a pretty penny and I suspicion most of us are a good degree poorer for our interest. But the truth is we bit off more'n we could chew, and we've got to face the fact. Some of us I know feel sore about the tactics of those who have fought us; and I can't say myself that I'm any too satisfied. But it has all been legal, so there's no redress. We just haven't the resources to carry on." Devoran paused and took a pinch of snuff.

Tonkin said: "You can form a company like this with fair enough prospects and find many people willing to invest a little. But it is altogether a different matter to find people willing to buttress up a shaky concern or to buy shares suddenly flung on the market. They see that the company is in difficulty and aren't agreeable to risk their money then."

Sir John Trevaunance said: "The company would have stood twice the chance if we had restricted it to people with unassailable credit."

Tonkin said: "You can't hold an inquiry into people's finances when they wish you well. And of course it was not thought that the exact composition of the company should ever become publicly known."

"Oh, you know what it is in these parts," Sir John remarked. "No man can keep a secret for five minutes. I do believe it is something in the air, it is moist and humid and breeds confidences."

"Well, somebody's confidences have

725

cost us dear," said Tonkin. "I have lost my position and best part of my life's savings."

"And I am for bankruptcy," said Harry Blewett. "Wheal Maid must close this month. It is doubtful if I will stay out of prison."

"Where is Penvenen to-night?" Ross asked.

There was silence.

Sir John said: "Well, don't look at me. I am not his keeper."

"He has lost interest in the sinking ship," Tonkin said rather bitterly.

"He is more interested in his rolling mill than in the copper company," Johnson said.

"As for a *sinking* ship," Sir John said, "I think in truth the ship may be considered sunk. There is no question of desertion. When one is left struggling in the water it is but natural to make what provision one can to reach dry land."

Ross had been watching the faces of his companions. There was the barest touch of complacency about Sir John that he had not noticed before Christmas. In this

venture Sir John stood to lose the most —
though not proportionately the most. The
great smelting furnaces stood on his land.
During the company's brief life he had
been the only one to receive a return for
his larger investment — in the shape of
port dues, increased profit from his coal
ships, ground rent and other items. This
change was therefore surprising. Had he
during Christmas caught sight of some
dry land not visible to the others?

All the time Ross had been striving to
sense the mood of the other men. He had
been hoping for signs of a greater
resilience in some of them. But even
Tonkin was resigned. Yet he was
determined to make a last effort to bring
them round.

"I don't altogether agree that the ship is
sunk yet," he said. "I have one suggestion
to make. It might just see us through the
difficult months until the spring. . . ."

Trenwith House looked chill and grey.
Perhaps it was only her imagination
harking back to the last visit. Or perhaps
it was knowing what the house now held.

She pulled at the front doorbell and fancied she heard it jangling somewhere away in the kitchens right across the inner court. The garden here was overgrown, and the lawn falling away to the stream and the pond was green and unkempt. Two curlews ran across it, dipping their tufted heads and sheering away as they saw her.

She pulled the bell again. Silence.

She tried the door. The big ring handle lifted the latch easily and the heavy door swung back with a creak.

There was nobody in the big hall. Although the tall mullioned window faced south the shadows of the winter afternoon were already heavy in the house. The rows of family pictures at the end and going up the stairs were all dark except for one. A shaft of pale light from the window fell on the portrait of the red-haired Anna-Maria Trenwith, who had been born, said Aunt Agatha, when Old Rowley was on the throne, whoever he might be. Her oval face and the fixed blue eyes stared out through the window and over the lawn.

Demelza shivered. Her finger touching

the long table came away dusty. There was a herby smell. She would have done better to follow her old custom and go round the back. At that moment a door banged somewhere upstairs.

She went across to the big parlour and tapped. The door was ajar and she pushed it open. The room was empty and cold and the furniture was hung in dust sheets.

So this was the part they were not using. Only two years ago she had come to this house for the first time, when Julia was on the way, had been sick and drunk five glasses of port and sung to a lot of ladies and gentlemen she had never seen before. John Treneglos had been there, merry with wine, and Ruth his spiteful wife, and George Warleggan; and dear Verity. This house had been glittering and candlelit then, enormous and as impressive to her as a palace in a fairy tale. Since then she had seen the Warleggans' town house, the Assembly Rooms, Werry House. She was experienced, adult and grown-up now. But she had been happier then.

She heard a footstep on the stairs and slipped back quickly into the hall.

In the half-light an old woman was tottering down them clutching anxiously at the banister. She was in faded black satin and wore a white shawl over her wig.

Demelza went quickly forward.

Aunt Agatha's ancient tremblings came to a stop. She peered at the girl, her eyes interred before their time in a mass of folds and wrinkles.

"What — eh . . . ? Is it you, Verity? Come back have ye? And about time too——"

"No, it's Demelza." She raised her voice. "Demelza, Ross's wife. I came to inquire."

"You what? Oh, yes, tis Ross's little bud. Well, this be no time for calling. They're all sick, every last jack of them. All except me and Mary Bartle. And she be so busy attending on them that she's no time to bother with a old woman. Let me starve! I b'lieve she would! Lord damme, don't an old body need just so much attention as a young?" She clung precariously to the banister and a tear tried to trickle down her cheek, but got diverted by a wrinkle. "Tis all bad managing, and that's a fact. Everything has gone amiss since Verity left. She never ought to have left, d'you hear. Twas selfish in her to go running after that man. Her duty was to stay. Her father always said so. She'd take no notice of me. Always headstrong, she was. I bring to mind when she was but five——''

Demelza slipped past her and ran up the stairs.

She knew where the main bedrooms were, and as she turned the corner of the corridor an elderly black-haired woman came out of one of the rooms carrying a bowl of water. Demelza recognized her as Aunt Sarah Tregeagle, Uncle Ben's putative wife. She dipped a brief curtsy when she saw Demelza.

''Are they in here?''

''Yes, ma'am.''

''Are you — seeing after them?''

''Well, Dr. Tommy calls me in, ma'am. But tis midwifing that belongs to be my proper work, as ye d'know. I come 'cos there was no one else. But my proper work be lying-in — or laying-out, when need be.''

Her hand on the door, Demelza stared after the woman, who was slopping water on the floor in her carelessness. Everyone knew Aunt Sarah. Not the nurse for these gentlefolk. But of course there was no choice. The smell of herbs was much stronger here.

She opened the door gently and slipped in.

After the meeting of the shareholders Ross did not go straight back to the Pascoes'. They did not sup till eight, and he did not want to spend an hour making polite conversation with the ladies in the parlour.

So he strolled through the back streets of the little town. Deliberately he turned his mind away from all the things which had just finished. Instead he thought about himself and his family, about his rake of a father, who had been in and out of trouble all his life, making love to one woman after another, fighting with this husband and that parent, cynical and disillusioned and sturdy to the end. He thought of Demelza and of how his estrangement from Francis sometimes seemed to come between her and him. It had no business to but it did — a sort of reservation, a bar sinister on their clear intimacy. He thought of Garrick her dog, of Julia, laughing and self-absorbed and untroubled with the perplexities of the world. He thought of Mark Daniel away in a foreign land, and wondered if he would ever bring himself to settle down there, or whether one day homesickness would lure him back into the shadow of the gibbet. He thought of the sickness at Trenwith and of Verity.

The drift of his steps had taken him out of the town and towards the river, which was full to-night and gleamed here and there with the lights of ships and lanterns moving about the docks. There were three vessels moored alongside the wharves: two small schooners and a ship of some size for this creek, a brigantine Ross saw when he got near enough to make out the yards on her foremast. She was a nice new ship, recently painted, with brass glistening on the poop. She would draw so much water, he thought, as to make it unsafe to put in and out of here except at the high tides. That was the reason for all the bustle to-night.

He strolled on towards the trees growing low to the riverbank and then turned to come back. From here, although there was no moon, you could make out the wide gleam of the flood tide with the masts like lattices in the foreground and the winking pins of light in the black rim of the town.

As he came near the brigantine again he saw several men going aboard. Two sailors held lanterns at the top of the gangway, and as one of the men reached the deck the lantern light fell clear on his face. Ross made a half movement and then checked himself. There was nothing he could do to this man.

He walked thoughtfully on. He turned back to look once, but the men had gone below. A sailor passed.

"Are you for the *Queen Charlotte?*" Ross asked on impulse.

The sailor stopped and peered suspiciously. "Me, sur? No, sur. *Fairy Vale.* Cap'n Hodges."

"She's a fine ship, the *Queen Charlotte,*" Ross said. "Is she new to these parts?"

"Oh, she's been in three or four times this year, I bla."

"Who is her master?"

"Cap'n Bray, sur. She's just off, I reckon."

"What is her cargo, do you know?"

"Grain for the most part: an' pilchards." The sailor moved on.

Ross stared at the ship a moment longer and then turned and walked back into the town.

The heavy smell of incense came from a little brazier of disinfectant herbs burning smokily in the centre of the bedroom. Demelza had found them all in the one room. Francis lay in the great mahogany bed. Geoffrey Charles was in his own small bed in the alcove. Elizabeth sat beside him.

Any resentment she might once have felt for Demelza was as nothing before relief at her coming now.

"Oh, Demelza, how kind of you! I have

been in — in despair. We are in — terrible straits. How kind of you. My poor little boy. . . ."

Demelza stared at the child. Geoffrey Charles was struggling for breath, every intake sounded raw and hoarse and painful. His face was flushed and strained and his eyes only half open. There were red spots behind his ears and on the nape of his neck. One hand kept opening and shutting as he breathed.

"He — he has these paroxysms," Elizabeth muttered. "And then he spits up or vomits; there is relief then; but only for — for a time before it begins all over again."

Her voice was broken and despairing. Demelza looked at her flushed face, at the piled fair hair, at the great glistening grey eyes.

"You're ill yourself, Elizabeth. You did ought to be in bed."

"A slight fever. But not this. I can manage to keep up. Oh, my poor boy. I have prayed — and prayed. . . ."

"And Francis?"

Elizabeth coughed and swallowed with

difficulty. "Is . . . a little . . . on the mend. There — there my poor dear . . . if only I could help him. We paint his throat with Melrose; but there seems small relief. . . ."

"Who is it?" said Francis from the bed. His voice was almost unrecognizable.

"It is Demelza. She has come to help us."

There was silence.

Then Francis said slowly: "It is good of her to overlook past quarrels. . . ."

Demelza breathed out a slow breath.

"If . . . the servants had not been ill too," Elizabeth went on, "we could have made a better shift. . . . But only Mary Bartle . . . Tom Choake has persuaded Aunt Sarah . . . It is not a pretty task . . . He could find no one else."

"Don't talk any more," Demelza said. "You should be abed. Look, Elizabeth, I — I didn't know if I came to stay for a long time, for I didn't know how you was fixed——"

"But——"

"But since you need me I'll stay — so long as ever I can. But first — soon —

soon I must slip home and tell Jane Gimlett and give her word for looking after Julia. Then I'll be back.''

"Thank you. If only for to-night. It is such a relief to have someone to rely on. Thank you again. Do you hear, Francis, Demelza is going to see us through to-night.''

The door opened and Aunt Sarah Tregeagle hobbled in with a bowl full of clean water.

"Aunt Sarah,'' said Demelza, "will you help me with Mrs. Poldark. She must be put to bed.''

After supper at the Pascoes', when the ladies had left them and they were settling to the port, Harris Pascoe said:

"Well; and what is your news to-day?''

Ross stared at the dark wine in his glass. "We are finished. The company will be wound up to-morrow.''

The banker shook his head.

"I made a last effort to persuade them otherwise,'' Ross said. "For the first time in years copper has moved up instead of down. I put that to them and suggested we should try to keep together for another six months. I suggested that the furnace workers should be invited to work on a profit-sharing basis. Every mine does the same thing when it strikes bargains with tributers. I suggested we should make one last effort. A few were willing but the influential men would have none of it."

"Especially S-Sir John Trevaunance," said the banker.

"Yes. How did you know?"

"You are right about the price of copper. I had news to-day, it has risen another three pounds."

"That is six pounds in six weeks."

"But, mind you, years may pass before the metal reaches an economic level."

"How did you know Sir John would be opposed to my suggestion?"

Harris Pascoe licked his lips and looked diffident.

"Not so much opposed to your suggestion in p-particular as to a continuance in general. And then I was rather going on hearsay."

"Which is?"

"Which is that — er — Sir John, after

battling against the wind for twelve months, is now preparing to sail with it. He has lost a tidy sum over this project and is anxious to recoup himself. He does not wish to see the smelting works lying idle permanently."

Ross thought of Sir John's voice that evening; he remembered Ray Penvenen's absence.

He got up. "Do you mean he is selling out to the Warleggans?"

The little banker reached for his wine.

"I think he is willing to come to some accommodation with them. Beyond that I know nothing."

"He and Penvenen are going to make a deal to cover their own losses while the rest of us go to the wall."

"I imagine it likely," said Pascoe, "that some sort of a caretaker company will be formed, and that the Warleggans will have a representative on it."

Ross was silent, staring at the books in the cabinet.

"Tell me," he said, "this evening I thought I saw Matthew Sanson boarding a ship in the docks. Could that be possible?"

"Yes, he has been back in Truro for several months."

"He is allowed to come back here and trade as if nothing had happened? Are the Warleggans complete masters of the district?"

"No one cares sufficiently about Sanson to make a fuss. There are only four or five people whom he cheated, and they are not influential."

"And the ship he sails in?"

"Yes, that is the property of a company controlled by the Warleggans. There's the *Queen Charlotte* and the *Lady Lyson*. No doubt they're a profitable side line."

Ross said: "If I were in your shoes I should tremble for my soul. Is there anyone besides you in the town they don't own from head to toe?"

Pascoe coloured. "I like them little more than you. But you're t-taking an extreme view now. The average man in the district only knows them as rich and influential people. You know them as something more because you chose to challenge them on their own ground. I am only sorry — profoundly sorry — that you have not been more successful. If g-good will would have sufficed you would have triumphed without a doubt."

"Whereas good will did not suffice," Ross said. "What we needed was good gold."

"It was not my project," said the banker, after a moment. "I did what I could and will be the poorer for it."

"I know," Ross said. "Failure puts an edge on one's tongue." He sat down again. "Well, now comes the reckoning. Let's get it over. The company will almost clear itself; so that leaves only our personal ends to be settled. What is my indebtedness to you?"

Harris Pascoe straightened his steel spectacles. "Not a big sum — about n-nine hundred pounds or a little less. That is over and above the mortgage on your property."

Ross said: "The sale of my Wheal Leisure shares will meet most of that — together with the dividend we have just declared."

"It will rather more than meet it. By chance I heard of someone inquiring for shares of Wheal Leisure only yesterday. They offered eight hundred and twenty-five pounds for sixty shares."

"There is one other small matter," Ross said. "Harry Blewett of Wheal Maid is worse hit than I am. He fears going to prison and I don't wonder. The shares and the dividend will come to nearly a thousand and I want the extra to go to him. It's possible that with it he'll be able to keep his head up."

"Then you wish me to sell the shares at that price?"

"If it's the best you can get."

"It is better than you would receive if they were thrown on the open market. Thirteen pounds fifteen shillings a share is a good price for these days."

"Thirteen pounds . . ." The wineglass suddenly snapped in Ross's fingers and the red wine splashed over his hand.

Pascoe was standing beside him. "What is wrong? Are you ill?"

"No," said Ross. "Not at all ill. Your glass has a delicate stem. I hope it was not an heirloom."

"No. But something . . ."

Ross said: "I have decided different. I do not sell the shares."

"It was a m-man called Coke who approached me. . . ."

Ross took out a handkerchief and wiped his hand. "It was a man called Warleggan."

"Oh, no, I assure you. What makes you——"

"I don't care what nominee they chose. It is their money and they shall not have the shares."

Pascoe looked a little put out as he handed Ross another glass. "I had no idea. I s-sympathize with your feeling. But it is a good offer."

"It will not be taken," Ross said. "Not if I have to sell the house and the land. I'm sorry, Harris; you'll wait for your money whether you like it nor not. You cannot force me for another month or so. Well, I'll get it before then — somehow. In the meantime, I'll keep my own mine smelling sweet if I go to gaol for it."

CHAPTER V

Mr. Notary Pearce was at home playing cribbage with his daughter when Ross was announced. Miss Pearce, a comely young woman of twenty-five who never made enough of her good looks, rose at once and excused herself, and Mr. Pearce, pushing aside the table, poked at the huge fire with his curtain rod and invited Ross to sit down.

"Well, Captain Poldark; I declare this is quite an event. Can you stay for a hand of cribbage? Playing with Grace is always a little dull, for she will not hazard a penny on the outcome."

Ross moved his chair farther from the fire.

"I need your advice and help."

"Well, my dear sir, you may have them if they are mine to give."

"I want a loan of a thousand pounds without security."

Mr. Pearce's eyebrows went up. Like other shareholders of Wheal Leisure, he had stood aloof from the battle of the copper companies. But he knew very well which way it had gone.

"Hrr-hm. That is rather a severe proposition. *Without* security, you said? Yes, I thought so. Dear, dear."

Ross said: "I should be willing to pay a high rate of interest."

Mr. Pearce scratched himself. *"Without* security. Have you tried Cary Warleggan?"

"No," said Ross. "Nor do I intend to."

"Just so. Just so. But it will be very difficult. If you have no security, what can you offer?"

"My word."

"Yes, yes. Yes, yes. But that would really amount to a friendly accommodation. Have you approached any of your friends?"

"No. I want it to be a business arrangement. I will pay for the privilege."

"You will pay? You mean in interest? Yes . . . But the lender might be chiefly concerned for his capital. Why do you not sell your shares in Wheal Leisure if you need the money so badly?"

"Because that is what I am trying to avoid."

"Ah, yes." Mr. Pearce's plum-coloured face was not encouraging. "And your property?"

"Is already mortgaged."

"For how much?"

Ross told him.

Mr. Pearce took a pinch of snuff. "I think the Warleggans would raise that figure if you transferred the mortgage to them."

"Several times in recent years," Ross said, "the Warleggans have tried to interest themselves in my affairs. I mean to keep them out."

It was on Mr. Pearce's tongue to say that beggars could not be choosers, but he changed his mind.

"Have you thought of a second mortgage on the property? There are people — I know one or two who might be willing for the speculative risk."

"Would that bring in sufficient?"

"It might. But naturally such a risk would be a short-term one, say for twelve or twenty-four months——"

"That would be agreeable."

"— and would carry a very high interest rate. In the nature of forty per cent."

For a loan of a thousand pounds now he would have to find fourteen hundred by this time next year, in addition to his other commitments. A hopeless proposition — unless the price of copper continued to rise and Wheal Leisure struck another lode as rich as the present.

"Could you arrange such a loan?"

"I could try. It is a bad time for such things. There is no cheap money about."

"That is not cheap money."

"No, no. I quite agree. Well, I could let you know in a day or two."

"I should want to know to-morrow."

Mr. Pearce struggled out of his chair. "Dear, dear, how stiff one gets. I have been better but there is still some gouty humour lurking in my constitution. I could let you know to-morrow possibly, though it might take a week or so to get the money."

"That will do," Ross said. "I'll take that."

On Tuesday he delayed leaving the town until five in the afternoon.

He and Johnson and Tonkin and Blewett wound up the Carnmore Copper Company before dinner. Ross did not pass on Harris Pascoe's hint of yesterday. There was nothing any of them could do now to prevent Sir John's entering into some agreement with the Warleggans if he chose to. There was nothing to prevent the smelting works from coming into the hands of the Warleggans or a new company being formed to exploit their own hard work. But the company would be one of the circle, and he would see that it did not force up prices for the benefit of the mines.

Although Tonkin was not ruined, Ross felt most sorry for him, for he liked him the best and knew the quite tireless work he had put in, arguing, persuading, contriving. Fifteen months of fanatical energy had gone into it, and he looked worn out. Harry Blewett, who had been the instigator and first supporter of the idea, had pledged his last penny, and today was the end of everything for him. The big, dour, hard-headed Johnson stood the failure more confidently than the others; he was a better loser because he had lost less.

After it was over Ross went to see Mr. Pearce again, and learned that the money was forthcoming. He wondered if Mr. Pearce himself had advanced it. The notary was an astute man and fast becoming a warm one.

Then Ross went back to the Pascoes. The banker shook his head at the news. Such improvident borrowing was utterly against his principles. Better by far to cut your losses and start again than to plunge so deep in that there might be no getting out — merely to put off the evil day.

While he was there Ross wrote to Blewett saying he had placed two hundred and fifty pounds to his name at Pascoe's Bank. This was to be considered a five-year loan at four per cent interest. He hoped it would tide him over.

The journey home in the dark took Ross about two hours. On the way down the dark combe, just before the lights of Nampara came in sight, he overtook a cloaked figure hurrying on ahead of him.

He had been feeling bitter and depressed, but at sight of Demelza he mustered up his spirits.

"Well, my dear. You are out late. Have you been visiting again?"

"Oh, Ross," she said. "I'm that glad you're not home before me. I was afraid you would have been."

"Is anything wrong?"

"No, no. I'll tell you when we're home."

"Come. Up beside me. It will save a half mile."

She put her foot on his and he lifted her up. Darkie gave a lurch. Demelza settled down in front of him with a sudden sigh of contentment.

"You should have someone with you if you intend to be abroad after dark."

"Oh . . . it is safe enough near home."

"Don't be too sure. There is too much poverty to breed all honest men."

"Have you saved anything, Ross. Is it to go on?"

He told her.

"Oh, my dear, I'm that sorry. Sorry for you. I don't belong to know how it has all happened. . . ."

"Never mind. The fever is over. Now we must settle down."

"What fever?" she asked in a startled voice.

He patted her arm. "It was a figure of speech. Have you heard that there is illness at Trenwith, by the way? I had intended to call to-day but I was so late."

"Yes. I heard . . . yesterday."

"Did you hear how they were?"

"Yes. They are a small bit better to-day — though not yet out of danger."

The house loomed ahead of them as they crossed the stream. At the door he got down and lifted her down. Affectionately he bent his head to kiss her, but in the dark she had moved her face slightly so that his lips found only her cheek.

She turned and opened the door. "John!" she called. "We're back!"

Supper was a quiet meal. Ross was going over the events of the last few days. Demelza was unusually silent. He had told her that he had saved his holding in Wheal Leisure, but not how. That would come when repayment was nearer. Sufficient unto the day.

He wished now he had kicked George Warleggan into the gutter while there was the opportunity: George was the type that was usually careful to avoid giving an excuse. And to have the impertinence to bring Cousin Sanson back. He wondered what Francis would have to say. Francis.

"Did you say Geoffrey Charles was better also?" he asked. "The sore throat is usually hard on children."

Demelza started and went on with her supper.

"I b'lieve the worst is over."

"Well, that is some satisfaction. I shall never have room for Francis again after the trick he served us; but I would not wish that complaint on my worst enemy."

There was a long silence.

"Ross," she said, "after July I swore I would never keep a secret from you again, so you had best hear this now before it can be thought I have deceived you."

"Oh," he said, "what? Have you been to see Verity in my absence?"

"No. To Trenwith."

She watched his expression. It did not change.

"To call, you mean?"

"No . . . I went to help."

A candle was smoking but neither of them moved to snuff it.

"And did they turn you away?"

"No. I stayed all last night."

He looked across the table at her. "Why?"

"Ross, I had to. I went to inquire, but they were in desperate straits. Francis — the fever had left him but he was prostrate. Geoffrey Charles was fit to die at any moment. Elizabeth had it too, though she would not admit it. There was three servants ill, and only Mary Bartle and Aunt Sarah Tregeagle to do anything. I helped to get Elizabeth to bed and stayed with Geoffrey Charles all night. I thought once or twice he was gone; but he brought round again and this morning was better.

I came home then an' went again this afternoon. Dr. Choake says the crisis is past. Elizabeth, he says, has not took it so bad. I — I stayed so long as ever I could, but I told them I could not stay to-night. But Tabb is up again and can see to the others. They will be able to manage to-night.''

He looked at her a moment. He was not a petty man, and the things that came to his lips were the things he could not say.

And, though at first he struggled to deny it, he could not in the end fail to acknowledge that the feeling moving in her had moved him no differently in the matter of Jim Carter. Could he blame her for the sort of impulse on which he had acted himself?

He could not subdue his thoughts, but honesty and the finer bonds of his affection kept him mute.

So the meal went on in silence.

At length she said: "I couldn't do any other, Ross."

"No," he said, "it was a kind and generous act. Perhaps in a fortnight I shall be in a mood to appreciate it."

They both knew what he meant but neither of them put it more clearly into words.

CHAPTER VI

A south-westerly gale broke during the night and blew for twenty hours. There was a brief quiet spell and then the wind got up again from the north, bitterly cold, and whipping rain and sleet and snow flurries before it. New Year's Day 1790, which was a Friday, dawned at the height of the gale.

They had gone to bed early as Demelza was tired. She had had a broken night before, Julia being fretful with teeth.

All night the wind thundered and screamed — with that thin, cold whistling scream which was a sure sign of a "norther." All night rain and hail thrashed on the windows facing the sea, and there were cloths laid along the window bottoms to catch the rain that was beaten in. It was cold even in bed with the curtains drawn, and Ross had made up a great fire in the parlour below to give a little extra heat. It was useless to light a fire in the bedroom grate, for all the smoke blew down the chimney.

Ross woke to the sound of Julia's crying. It reached very thinly to him for the wind was rampant, and he decided, as Demelza had not heard, to slip out himself and see if he could quiet the child. He sat up slowly; and then knew that Demelza was not beside him.

He parted the curtains, and the cold draught of the wind wafted upon his face. Demelza was sitting by the cot. A candle dripped and guttered on the table near. He made a little hissing sound to attract her attention, and she turned her head.

"What is it?" he asked.

"I don't rightly know, Ross. The teeth, I b'lieve."

"You will catch a consumption sitting there. Put on your gown."

"No, I am not cold."

"*She* is cold. Bring her into this bed."

Her answer was drowned by a sudden storm of hail on the window. It stopped all talk. He got out of bed, struggled into his gown and took up hers. He went over to her and put it about her shoulders. They peered down at the child.

Julia was awake but her plump little face was flushed, and when she cried her whimper seemed to end in a sudden dry cough.

"She has a fever," Ross shouted.

"I think it is a teething fever, I think . . . ."

The hail stopped as suddenly as it had begun and the scream of the wind seemed like silence after it.

"It will be as well to have her with us to-night," Demelza said. She bent forward, it seemed to him, and picked up the child. Her dressing gown slipped off and lay on the floor.

He followed her back to the bed and they put Julia in it.

"I will just get a drink of water," she said.

He watched her go over to the jug and pour some out. She drank a little slowly, and took some more. Her shadow lurched and eddied on the wall. Suddenly he was up beside her.

"What is the matter?"

She looked at him. "I think I have caught a cold."

He put a hand on hers. Although the icy breeze was in the room her hand was hot and sweaty.

"How long have you been like this?"

"All night. I felt it coming last evening."

He stared at her. In the shadowed light he could see her face. He caught at the high frilly collar of her nightdress and pulled it back.

"Your neck is swollen," he said.

She stepped back from him and buried her face in her hands.

"My head," she whispered, "is that bad."

He had roused the Gimletts. He had carried the child and Demelza down into the parlour and wrapped them in blankets before the drowsy fire. Gimlett he had sent for Dwight. Mrs. Gimlett was making up the bed in Joshua's old room. There there was a fire grate which would not smoke, and the only window faced south; a more habitable sick-room in such a gale.

He found time to be grateful for having changed the Paynters for the Gimletts. No grudging grumbling service, no self-pitying lamentation on their own ill luck.

While he sat there talking in the parlour, talking softly to Demelza and telling her that Julia was a sturdy child and would come through quick enough, his mind was full of bitter thoughts. They flooded over him in waves, threatening to crown common sense and cool reason. He could have torn at himself in his distress. Demelza had run her head recklessly into the noose. The obligations of relationship . . .

No, not that. Although he could not see through to the source of her generous impulses, he knew it was much more than that. All these things were tied together in her heart; her share in Verity's flight, his quarrel with Francis, his quarrel with her, the failure of the copper company, her visit to the sick house of Trenwith. They could not be seen separately, and in a queer way the responsibility for her illness now seemed not only hers but his.

But he had not shown his anxiety or resentment three days ago; he could not possibly show it now. Instead he wiped her forehead and joked with her and watched over Julia, who slept now after a bout of crying.

Presently he went out to help Jane Gimlett. A fire was burning already in the downstairs bedroom, and he saw that Jane had stripped the bed upstairs to make up this one so that there should be no risk of damp. While he was helping Demelza to bed the whole house echoed and drummed, carpets flapped and pictures rattled. Then the front door was shut again and Dwight Enys was taking off his wet cloak in the hall.

He came through and Ross held a candle while he examined Demelza's throat; he timed her heart with his pulse watch, asked one or two questions, turned to the child. Demelza lay quiet in the great box bed and watched him. After a few minutes he went out into the hall for his bag, and Ross followed him.

"Well?" said Ross.

"They both have it."

"You mean the malignant sore throat?"

"The symptoms are unmistakable. Your wife's are further advanced than the baby's. Even to the pink finger ends."

Dwight would have avoided his eyes and gone back into the room but Ross stopped him.

"How bad is this going to be?"

"I don't know, Ross. Some get past the acute stage quick, but recovery is always a long job, three to six weeks."

"Oh, the length of recovery is nothing," Ross said.

Dwight patted his arm. "I know that. I know."

"The treatment?"

"There is little we can do: so much hangs on the patient. I have had some success with milk — boiled, always boiled, and allowed to cool until it is tepid. It sustains the patient. No solids. Keep them very flat, and no exertion or excitement. The heart should have the least possible work. Perhaps some spirits of sea salt painted on the throat. I do not believe in bloodletting."

"Does the crisis come soon?"

"No, no. A day or two. In the meantime be patient and have a good heart. They stand so much better a chance than the cottage people, who are half starved and usually without fire and light."

"Yes," said Ross, remembering Dwight's words a few mornings before. "The results are always unpredictable," he had said. "Sometimes the strong will go and the weak survive."

CHAPTER VII

The northerly gale blew for three days more.

In the late part of New Year's Day snow began to blow in flurries before the wind, and by next morning there were drifts of it against all the hedges and walls, though the gale-swept ground was free. The pump in the yard was hung with tattered icicles like a beggar woman, and the water in the pail was frozen. The clouds were livid and low.

In the middle of the day the hail began again. It seemed hardly to fall at all but to blow flatly across the land. One felt that no glass would withstand it. Then it would rap, rap, rap a dozen times and suddenly stop and one could hear the wind like a roaring mighty beast rolling away in the distance.

To Demelza all the noise and fury was a true part of her nightmare. For two days her fever was high, and something in being in old Joshua's big box bed threw her errant mind back to the first night she had ever spent at Nampara. The years slipped off and she was a child of thirteen again, ragged, ill fed, ignorant, half cheeky, half terrified. She had been stripped and swilled under the pump and draped in a lavender-smelling shirt and put to sleep in this great bed. The weals of her father's latest thrashing were still sore on her back, her ribs ached from the kicks of the urchins of Redruth Fair. The candle smoked and guttered on the bedside table and the painted statuette of the Virgin nodded down at her from the mantelpiece. To make things worse she could not swallow, for someone had tied a cord about her throat; and there was Someone waiting behind the library door until she fell asleep and the candle went out, when they would creep in in the dark and tighten the knot.

So she must stay awake, at all costs she must stay awake. Very soon Garrick would come scratching at the window, and then she must go to open it and let him in. He would be a comfort and a protection through the night.

Sometimes people moved about the room, and often she saw Ross and Jane Gimlett and young Dr. Enys. They were there, but they were not real. Not even the child in the cot, her child, was real. They were the imagination, the dream, something to do with an impossible future, something she hoped for but had never had. The *now* lay in the guttering candle and the nodding statuette and the aching ribs and the cord round her throat and the Someone waiting behind the library door.

"Ye've slocked my dattur!" shouted Tom Carne, while she trembled in the cupboard. "What right ha' you to be seein' her back! I'll have the law on you!"

"That statuette seems to be worrying her," Ross said. "I wonder if it would be wise to move it."

She looked over the edge of the bed, out of the cupboard, down, down, to two tiny figures fighting on the floor far below her.

Ross had thrown her father into the fireplace but he was getting up again. He was going to put something round her throat.

"Are ye saved?" he whispered. "Are ye saved? Sin an' fornication an' drunkenness. The Lord hath brought me out of a horrible pit of mire an' clay an' set my feet 'pon a rock. There's no more drinkings an' living in sin."

"Saved?" said Francis. "Saved from what?" And every one tittered. They weren't laughing at Francis but at her, for trying to put on airs and pretending to be one of them, when she was really only a kitchen wench dragged up in a lice-ridden cottage. Kitchen wench. Kitchen wench. . . .

"Oh," she said with a great sigh, and threw her life and her memories away, out over the edge of the bed into the sea. They fell, twirling, twisting away, growing ever smaller, smaller. Let them drown. Let them perish and die, if she could but have peace.

"Let him drown in the mud," Ross said. "Cheating at cards — let him drown."

"No, Ross, no, Ross, no!" She grasped his arm. "Save him. Else they'll say tis murder. What does it matter so long as we've got back what we lost. So long as we haven't lost Wheal Leisure. We'll be together again. That is all that counts."

She shrank from the touch of something cool on her forehead.

"It's unusual for the fever to persist so long," said Dwight. "I confess I am at a loss to know what to do."

Of course Mark had killed Keren this way. The men had not told her, but word had gone round. Against the window somehow, and then he had choked the life out of her. They were trying to do that now to her. She had been dozing and Someone had come in from the library and was just tightening the cord.

"Garrick!" she whispered. "Garrick! Here, boy! Help me now!"

"Drink this, my darling." Ross's voice came from a long way away, from the other room, from the room that was not hers, echoing out of her dreams.

"It is useless," said Dwight. "She can't swallow anything at present. In a few hours perhaps, if . . ."

Garrick was already scratching, eagerly scratching.

"Open the window!" she urged. "Open quick, afore tis . . . too . . . late."

Something large and black and shaggy bounded across the room to her, and with a gasp of joy she knew that they had done as she said. Her face and hands were licked by his rough tongue. She wept for sheer relief. But suddenly to her horror she found that the dog had somehow made a horrible mistake. Instead of knowing it was his mistress he thought she was an enemy and fastened his teeth in her throat. She struggled and fought to explain, but her voice and her breath were gone, were gone. . . .

The candle had blown out and it was cold. She shivered in the dark. Julia was crying with her teeth again, and she must get up and give her a drink of water. If only the wind was not so cold. Where was Ross? Had he not come back? He takes things so much to heart, Verity said, he takes things to heart. Well, then, I must not disappoint him this time. Deceived him once. Deceived him. I must not let him down. Clear, clear, but how might it happen? If you don't know you can't be sure.

Something with Julia and herself. But of course, Julia was sick. She had been watching by her bed all night. Francis was sick too, and Elizabeth was sick if she would only admit it. There was a horrible taste of copper in her mouth. It was those herbs they were burning. Aunt Sarah Tregeagle had come straight from carol singing to tend on them all. But where was . . .

"Ross!" she called. "Ross!"

"He's gone to sleep in his chair in the parlour, ma'am," said a woman's voice. It was not Prudie. "Do you want for me to call him? He's been without sleep these three nights."

It would not do for any of them to be asleep if her father came. He would bring all the Illuggan miners and they would set fire to the house. But he had reformed. He was a new man altogether. He had married Aunt Mary Chegwidden. How would he come this time, then? Perhaps with a choir of Methodists and they would sing outside the window. It seemed funny, and she tried to laugh but choked. And then she knew it was *not* funny, for *there* they were outside the window, there as she looked down on them, a great sea of faces. And she knew that they were hungry and wanted bread.

They were in a huge crowd stretching right up the valley and shouting. "Our right be bread t'eat an' corn to buy at a fair an' proper price. We want corn to live by, an' corn we'll have, whether or no!"

And she realized that the only bread she could give them was her own child. . . .

Beside her was Sanson, the miller; and Verity and Andrew Blamey were talking in the corner, but they were too lost in each other to notice her. She wept in an agony of fear. For the miners were crazy for bread. In a minute they would set fire to the house.

She turned to look for Ross, and when she turned back to the window the massed, staring tiny faces were already falling behind dense columns of white smoke.

"Look," said Jane Gimlett, "it is snowing again."

"Snowing!" she tried to say. "Don't you see, it is not snow but smoke. The house is on fire and we shall be smothered to death!" She saw Sanson fall and then felt the smoke getting into her own breath.

Choking, she put up a hand to her throat and found that someone else's hand was already there.

On the morning of January the fourth the wind broke and it began to snow in earnest. By midday, when the fall ceased, the fields and the trees were thick and heavy with it. Branches bowed and thick floes drifted down the stream. John Gimlett splitting wood in the yard had to tug at the logs to get them apart, for the cold had bound them tight. Gimlett's nine ducks padding laboriously towards the water looked dirty and jaundiced in this purity. On Hendrawna Beach the tide was out and the great waves leaped and roared in the distance. The ice and foam and yellow scum which had covered the beach for a week was itself overlaid by the cloth of snow. Sand hills were mountain ranges, and in the distance the dark cliffs brooded over the scene, wearing their new dress like a shroud.

The hush everywhere was profound. After the fanatic ravings of the gale it was as if a blanket had fallen on the world. Nothing stirred and a dog's bark echoed round the valley. The roar of the sea was there but had somehow become lost in the silence and could only be heard by an effort of thought.

Then at two the clouds broke up and the sun came out dazzlingly brilliant, forcing a brief thaw. Branches and bushes dripped, and small avalanches of snow, already part thawed from within, began to slip down the roof. Dark stains showed on one or two of the fields, and a robin, sitting among the feathery snow of an apple branch, began to sing to the sun.

But the break had come late in the day, and soon the valley was streaked with shadow and the frost had set in again.

About four o'clock, as it was getting dark, Demelza opened her eyes and looked up at the wooden ceiling of the bed. She felt different from before, calmer and quite separate. She was no longer the child of nightmare. There was only the one reality and that was of this moment of waking to the long smooth shadows in the room, to the livid glimmering paleness of the ceiling, to the curtains drawn back from the latticed windows, to Jane Gimlett nodding sleepily in the glow of an old peat fire.

She wondered what day it was, what time of day, what kind of weather. Some noise had stopped; was it in her head or out in the world? Everything was very peaceful and unemphatic, as if she looked at it from a distance, no longer belonged to it. All life and energy was spent. Was she too spent? Where was Ross? And Julia? Had they all been ill? She was not clear on that. She would have liked to speak but somehow was afraid to try. In speaking she either broke the shell of quiet in which she lay, or stayed within it for ever. That was at the very heart of the choice. She did not know and was afraid to try. And Jud and Prudie, and her father and Verity and Francis . . . No, no, stop;

that way, down that turning lay the nightmare.

Just then some of the peat fell in and caused a sharp glow and heat to fall on Jane Gimlett's face. She woke, sighed and yawned, put on more fuel. Presently she got up from her seat and came over to the bed to glance at the patient. What she saw there made her leave the room in search of Ross.

She found him slumped in his chair in the parlour staring into the fire.

They came back together and Ross went over alone to the bed.

Demelza's eyes were closed, but after a moment she seemed to feel the shadow across her face. She looked up and saw Ross. Jane Gimlett came to the bed with a candle and put it on the bedside table.

"Well, my love," said Ross.

Demelza tried to smile, and after a moment's frightened hesitancy took the risk of trying her voice.

"Well, Ross . . ."

The shell was broke. He had heard. Somehow she knew then she was going to get better.

She said something that he did not catch; he bent to hear it and again could not.

Then she said quite clearly: "Julia . . ."

"All right, my darling," he said. "But not now. To-morrow. When you're stronger. You shall see her then." He bent and kissed her forehead. "You must sleep now."

"Day?" she said.

"You've been ill a day or two," he said. "It has been snowing and is cold. Go to sleep now. Dwight is coming to see you again this evening and we want you to show improvement. Go to sleep, Demelza."

"Julia," she said.

"To-morrow. See her then, my love. Go to sleep."

Obedient, she closed her eyes and presently began to breathe more deeply and more slowly than he had seen her do for five days. He went over and stood by the window, wondering if he had done right to lie to her.

For Julia had died the night before.

CHAPTER VIII

They buried the child two days later. The weather had stayed quiet and cold, and heaps of snow lay in sheltered corners about the fields and lanes. A great number of people turned out for the funeral. Six young girls dressed in white — two Martins, Paul Daniel's daughters, and two of Jim Carter's younger sisters — carried the small coffin the whole of the mile and a half to Sawle Church, and all the way along the route were people who stood silently by and then quietly fell in behind the other followers to the church. Sawle choir, uninvited, met the procession halfway, and each time the six girls stopped to rest they sang a psalm, in which the mourners joined.

Dwight Enys walked with Ross, and behind them were John Treneglos and Sir

Hugh Bodrugan. Harry Blewett and Richard Tonkin had come, and Harris Pascoe had sent his eldest son. Captain and Mrs. Henshawe followed Joan Teague with one of the cousins Tremenheer. Behind them were Jud and Prudie Paynter, all the rest of the Martins and Daniels and Carters, the Viguses and the Nanfans, and then followed a great mass of ragged miners and their wives, small farmers and farm labourers, spallers, wheelwrights, fishermen. The sound of all these people singing psalms in the still, frosty air was very impressive. When they finished and before the shuffling movement of the procession began again, there was each time a brief hush when everyone heard the distant roar of the sea. In the end Mr. Odgers found he had to read the burial service before more than three hundred and fifty people, overflowing the church and standing silent in the churchyard.

It was this unexpected tribute that broke Ross up. He had hardened himself to all the rest. Not being a religious man, he had no resources to meet the loss of the child except his own resentful will. Inwardly he railed against Heaven and circumstance, but the very cruelty of the blow touched his character at its toughest and most obstinate.

That Demelza was likely to live did not in this early stage strike him as cause for thankfulness. The one loss had shocked and shaken him too much. When his mother had taken him to church as a child he had repeated a psalm which said: "To-day if ye will hear His voice, harden not your hearts." But when his mother died, even while he was crying, something within him had risen up, a barrier to shield off his weakness and tenderness and frailty. He had thought: All right, then, I've lost her and I'm alone. All right then. To-day the adult impulse followed the childish.

But the curious silent testimony of respect and affection given to-day by all these ordinary working or half-starving neighbours of his, turning out from field and farm and mine, had somehow slipped through his defences.

That night the gale blew up again from

the north, and all the evening he sat with Demelza. After a collapse when they broke the news to her yesterday she was slowly regaining the lost ground. It was as if nature, bent on its own survival, had not allowed her tired brain strength to dwell on her loss. The one thing it was concerned with was preserving her body. When the serious illness was really over, when the convalescence began, then would be the testing time.

About nine Dwight came again and after he had seen Demelza they sat in the parlour for a time.

Ross was brooding, inattentive, did not seem to follow the simplest remark. He kept on repeating how sorry he was he had not asked the mourners in for food and wine after the funeral. It was the custom in this part of the world, he explained, as if Dwight did not know, to give people food to eat and wine to drink and plenty of it at a funeral. The whole countryside had turned out to-day, he couldn't get over that; he had not expected it at all and hoped they would see that with Demelza still so ill, things couldn't be done as they should have been.

Dwight thought he had been drinking. In fact he was wrong. Since the third day of their illness Ross had lost the taste. The only physical thing wrong with him was lack of sleep.

There was something mentally wrong with him, but Dwight could do nothing for that. Only time or chance or Ross himself could set things to rights there. He could find no submission in defeat. If he was to regain his balance there must be some recoil of the spring of his nature, which had been pressed back within itself unbearably.

Dwight said: "Ross, I have not said this before, but I feel I must say it sometime. It is how acutely I feel it that I was not able to save — her."

Ross said: "I had not expected to see Sir Hugh to-day. He has more compassion in him than I thought."

"I feel I should have tried something else — anything. You brought me into this district. You have been a good friend all through. If I could have repaid that . . ."

"There was none from Trenwith at the

funeral," said Ross. "I expect they are all still unwell."

"Oh, if they have had this they will not be out for weeks. I have seen so much of this during last summer and autumn. I wish so much . . . Choake will no doubt say it was due to some neglect on my part. He will say that he saved Geoffrey Charles——"

"Demelza saved Geoffrey Charles," Ross said, "and gave Julia in his place."

The gale buffeted tremendously against the house.

Dwight got up. "You must feel that. I'm sorry."

"God, how this wind blows!" Ross said savagely.

"Would you like me to stay to-night?"

"No. You need the sleep also and need your strength for to-morrow. I can spend all this year at recovery. Take a hot drink and then go."

Ross put a kettle on the fire and had soon mixed a jug of grog, which they drank together.

Ross said: "They were a poor lot at the funeral, Dwight. I wish I could have fed and wined them after. They needed it."

"You could not be expected to victual the better part of three villages," Dwight said patiently.

There was a tap on the door.

"Beg pardon, sir," said Jane Gimlett, "but Mistress is asking for you to come and see her."

"Is anything wrong?"

"No, sur."

When Dwight had gone Ross went into the bedroom. Demelza looked very slight and pale in the big bed. She stretched out her hand and he took it and sat on the chair beside her.

Two candles flickered on the table, and the fire smouldered and glowed in the grate. Ross tried to find something to say.

"We had a letter from Verity this forenoon. I don't know what has become of it."

"Is — she — well?"

"Seems so, yes. I will read it you when it comes to light. She was inquiring for Francis and family. She had only just heard that there was some sort of sickness in the house."

"And us?"

". . . She had not heard about us."

"You — must write, Ross. An' tell her."

"I will."

"How are they . . . Ross? Elizabeth and . . ."

"Ill, but improving." He nearly added: "Even Geoffrey Charles," but killed his bitterness. Above all, there must never be any of that. He leaned his head against the wooden side of the bed and tried to forget all that had passed in these last weeks, all the frustration and the pain, tried to think himself back to the happy days of a year ago. So they sat for a long time. The wind was backing a little, would probably blow itself out in the north-west. The fire sank lower, and now and then the candles ducked and trembled.

He moved his hand a little, and at once she caught it more firmly in hers.

"I was not leaving you," he said, "except to stir the fire."

"Let it stay, Ross. Don't go just now. Don't leave me."

"What is it?" he asked.

"I was . . . only thinking."

"What?"

"That Julia — will be lonely. She always so hated the wind."

Ross stayed beside the bed all night. He did not sleep much but dozed fitfully off and on, while the wind buffeted and screamed. Awake and asleep the same thoughts lived in his brain. Frustration and bereavement. Jim Carter and the Warleggans and Julia. Failure and loss. His father dying untended in this same room. His own return from America, his disappointment over Elizabeth and happiness with Demelza. Was all that last joy gone? Perhaps not, but it would have changed its tone, and would be edged with memories. And his own life; what did it add up to? A frenzied futile struggle ending in failure and near bankruptcy. A part of his life was ended too, a phase, an epoch, a turning, and he could not see himself starting again along the same track. What had ended with this phase? Was it his youth?

How would he feel to-night if everything had happened different, if he had triumphed over the prison authorities and the Warleggans and disease and was not bereaved and beaten, lightheaded and tired to death? He would have been asleep and safe from these thoughts. Yet would the phase have ended just the same? He did not know and was too down to care. It did not seem just then that success in anything had ever been possible or that anything would ever be possible again. Failure was the end of life, all effort was dust, necessary and complete. All roads led to the bleak parapet of death.

In the cold gale of the early morning he fetched more wood, piled the fire high and then drank several glasses of brandy to keep out the chill. When he sat down again beside the bed the spirit seemed to set fire to his brain and he fell asleep.

He dreamed fantastic things, in which stress and conflict and the will to fight were all that meant anything: he lived over again in a few moments a concentrate of all the trouble of the last month and climbed back to wakefulness slowly, to find a grey daylight filtering through the curtains and John Gimlett bending before the fire.

"What time is it?" Ross asked in a whisper.

John turned. "About fifteen minutes before eight, sur, and there's a ship drifting in on the beach."

Ross turned and looked at Demelza. She was sleeping peacefully, her tumbled hair about the pillow; but he wished she did not look so white.

"Tes 'ardly light enough to see him proper yet, sur," whispered Gimlett. "I did but notice him when I went for the wood. I do not think any other has spied him so far."

"Eh?"

"The ship, sur. He looks a tidy size."

Ross reached for the brandy bottle and drank another glass. He was stiff and cold and his mouth was dry.

"Where away?"

"Just b'low Damsel Point. He cleared the point but he'll never get out o' the bay in this wind an' sea."

Ross's brain was still working slowly but the new brandy was having effect. There would be pickings for the miners and their families. Good luck to them.

"I b'lieve ye could see him from an upstairs window by now."

Ross got up and stretched. Then he went out of the room and listlessly climbed the stairs. The north window of their old bedroom was so thick with salt that he could see nothing at all, but when he had got it open he soon made out what Gimlett meant. A two-masted ship of fair size. She was dipping and lurching in the trough of the waves. All her sails were gone except a few strips flying in the wind, but some sort of a jury rig had been put up forward and they were trying to keep way on her. Unless she grew wings she would be on the beach soon. It was low water.

Losing interest, he was about to turn away, when something took his attention again and he stared at the ship. Then he went for his father's spyglass and steadied it against the frame of the window. It was a good glass, which his father had had in some bargain from a drunken frigate captain at Plymouth. As he peered the billowing curtains blew and flapped about his head. The wind was dropping at last.

Then he lowered the glass. The ship was the *Queen Charlotte.*

He went down. In the parlour he poured out a drink.

"John!" he called, as Gimlett went past.

"Please?"

"Get Darkie saddled."

Gimlett glanced up. In his master's eyes was a light as if he had seen a vision. But not a holy one.

"Are you feeling slight, sur?"

Ross drained another glass. "Those people at the funeral, John. They should have been entertained and fed. We must see that they are this morning."

Gimlett looked at him in alarm. "Sit you down, sur. There's no need for taking on any more."

"Get Darkie at once, John."

"But——"

Ross met his glance, and Gimlett went quickly away.

In the bedroom Demelza was still quietly sleeping. He put on his cloak and hat and mounted the horse as it came to the door. Darkie had been confined and was mettlesome, could hardly be contained. In a moment they were flying off up the valley.

The first cottage of Grambler village was dark and unstirring when Ross slithered up to it. Jud and Prudie had had smuggled gin in the house and, finding no free drink outcoming from the funeral, had returned, complaining bitterly, to make a night of it on their own.

Knocking brought no response so he put his shoulders to the door and snapped the flimsy bolt. In the dark and the stink he shook someone's shoulder, recognized it as Prudie's, tried again and scored a hit.

"Gor damme," shouted Jud, quivering with self-pity, "a man's not king of his own blathering 'ouse but what folks burst in——"

"Jud," said Ross quietly, "there's a wreck."

"Eh?" Jud sat up, suddenly quiet. "Where's she struck?"

"Hendrawna Beach. Any moment now. Go rouse Grambler people and send word to Mellin and Marasanvose. I am on to Sawle."

Jud squinted in the half-light, the bald top of his head looking like another face. "Why for bring all they? They'll be thur soon enough. Now ef——"

"She's a sizeable ship," Ross said. "Carrying food. There'll be pickings for all."

"Aye, but——"

"Do as I say, or I'll bolt you in here from the outside and do the job myself."

"I'll do en, Cap'n. Twas only as you might say a passing thought, like. What is she?"

Ross went out, slamming the door behind him so that the whole crazy cottage shook. A piece of dried mud fell from the roof upon Prudie's face.

"What's amiss wi' you!" She hit Jud across the head and sat up.

Jud sat there scratching inside his shirt.

"Twas some queer, that," he said. "Twas some queer, I tell ee."

"What? What's took you, wakin' at this time?"

"I was dreamin' of old Joshua," said

Jud. "Thur he was as clear as spit, just like I seen un in 'seventy-seven, when he went after that little giglet at St. Ives. An' damme, ef I didn't wake up an' *thur* he was standin' beside the bed, plain as plain."

"Who?"

"Old Joshua."

"You big soft ape, he's been cold in 'is grave these six year an' more!"

"Aye, twas Cap'n Ross, really."

"Then load me, why don't ee say so!"

"Because," said Jud, "I've never seen 'im look so much like old Joshua before."

CHAPTER IX

By superb seamanship Captain Bray kept her off the beach for over an hour.

In this he was helped by the lull in the storm, and once there even seemed a chance that he would fight his way clear.

But then the tide began to flow strongly and all was lost. Ross was home again just in time to see her come in.

He remembered the scene years after. Although the tide was out the sand was wet and foam-covered right up to the sand hills and the shingle. In places the cliffs were grey to the top with foam, and suds whirled in flocks between the cliffs like gulls wheeling. Along the edge of the sea proper a black rim of thirty or forty people were already come at his summons for the harvest. Riding in quickly, stern foremost, racked and tossed and half smothered by the sea, was the *Queen Charlotte*. As Ross climbed the wall the sun sprang up out of the broken black clouds fleeing to the east. A sickly unearthly yellow lit the sky, and the mountainous waves were tarnished with flecks of gold light. Then the sun was swallowed up in a tattered curtain of cloud and the light died.

She struck stern first as her captain aimed to do, but did not run in firm enough and a side wash lurching in a great pyramid across the tide broke over her and slewed her round broadside. In a few seconds she had heeled over, her decks facing the shore and the waves spouting.

Ross ran across the beach, drunkenly in the gusts; she had come ashore midway up, just this side of Leisure Cliff.

There was no chance of reaching her yet, but she was quickly being washed in. The waves had a tremendous run on them, would flood in halfway to the sand hills and then go out, leaving great glassy areas of water a half inch deep.

The men on board were trying to launch a boat. This was the worst thing, but on an incoming tide they stood no better chance by staying in the ship.

They lowered her from the well deck and set her in the water without mishap, and then, with only three or four in, a flood of water swirled round the lee side of the brigantine and swept the small boat away. The men rowed frantically to keep within the shelter, but they were as in a tide race and were borne quite clear. A wave rushed on them, and, smothered in water, they were carried inshore. Then they were left behind in the trough, and the next wave turned the boat upside down and broke it to pieces.

The men on shore had given way before the tide, but as the bigger waves passed, Ross and a few others stood staring out at the wreck while the retreating water rushed past their knees trying to carry them along.

"We'll not get to un this morning," said Vigus, rubbing his hands and shivering with cold. "Tide'll break un to bits, an' we shall have the pickings on the ebb. Might just so well go home."

"I can't see one o' they men," said

Zacky Martin. "I expect they've been sucked under and'll be spewed out farther downcoast."

"She'll not stand in this sea even for one tide," Ross said. "There'll be pickings soon enough."

Zacky glanced at him. There was a savagery in Ross this morning.

"Look fur yourself!" someone shouted.

An immense wave had hit the wreck and in a second a straight stiff column of spray stood two hundred feet in the air, to collapse slowly and disintegrate before the wind. Two men grasped Ross and dragged him back.

"She's going over!" he shouted.

They tried to run but could not. The wave caught them waist-high, swept them before it like straws; they were carried part way up the beach and left behind struggling in two feet of water, while the wave rushed on to spend its strength. There was just time to gain a foothold and brace themselves against the sudden rush back again. Ross wiped the water out of his eyes.

The *Queen Charlotte* could not last now.

The great weight of the wave had not only carried her in; it had almost turned her bottom up, snapping off both masts and washing away all but one or two of the crew. Spars and tangles of wreckage, barrels and masts, coils of rope and sacks of corn were bobbing in the surf.

People streaming down to the scene carried axes and baskets and empty sacks. They were a spur to those who were before them, and soon the shallow surf was black with people struggling to reach what they could. The tide washed in everything it could strip away. One of the crew had come ashore alive, three dead, the rest had gone.

As the morning grew and the day cleared more people came, with mules, ponies, dogs to carry away the stuff. But only a small part of the cargo was yet ashore, and there was not enough to go round. Ross made the people divide the spoils. If a barrel of pilchards came in it was broken open and doled out, a basketful to everyone who came. He was everywhere, ordering, advising, encouraging.

At ten three kegs of rum and one of brandy came in together and were at once opened. With hot spirit inside them men grew reckless and some even fought and struggled together in the water. As the tide rose, some fell back into the sand hills and lit bonfires from the wreckage and began a carouse. Newcomers plunged into the surf. Sometimes men and women were caught in the outrun of a wave and went tobogganing back into the sea. One was drowned.

At noon they were driven off most of the beach and watched the pounding of the hulk from a distance. Ross went back to Nampara, had something to eat, drank a great deal and was out again. He was gentle in reply to Demelza's questionings but unmoved.

A part of the deck had given way and more sacks of corn were coming in. Frantic that these should be taken before all the corn was spoiled, many had rushed down again, and as he followed them Ross passed the successful ones coming away. A great dripping sack of flour staggered slowly up the hill and under it, sweating and red-faced, was Mrs. Zacky. Aunt Betsy Triggs led a half-starved mule, laden with baskets of pilchards and a sack of corn. Old Man Daniel helped Beth Daniel with a table and two chairs. Jope Ishbel and Whitehead Scoble dragged a dead pig. Others carried firewood, one a basket of dripping coal.

On the beach Ross found men trying to loop a rope over a piece of hatchway which the sea was carrying out again. Restless, unsatisfied, trying to forget his own hurt, he went down to join them.

By two-thirty the tide had been ebbing an hour and nearly five hundred people waited. Another hundred danced and sang around the fires on the sand hills or lay drinking above high water. Not a piece of driftwood or a broken spar lay anywhere. Rumour had whispered that the Illuggan and St. Ann's miners were coming to claim a share. This lent urgency where none was needed.

At three Ross waded out into the surf. He had been wet on and off all day, and the stinging cold of the water did not strike him now.

It was bad going out — unless the sea malevolently chose to take you — but when he judged himself far enough he dived into a wave and swam underwater. He came up to face one that nearly flung him back on shore, but after a while he began to make headway. Once in the lee of the wreck he swam up and grasped the splintered spar which had once been the main mast and now stuck out towards the shore. He hauled himself up; men on shore shouted and waved soundlessly.

Not safe yet to climb to the high side of the deck. He untied the rope about his waist and hitched it to the root of the mast. A raised hand was a signal to the shore, and the rope quivered and tautened. In a few minutes there would be a score of others aboard with axes and saws.

Still astride the mast, he glanced about the ship. No sign of life. All the forecastle had given way and it was from here that the cargo had come. There would be pickings astern. He glanced at the poop. A different sight now from Truro Creek. All this week of gales and blizzard she must have been beating about in the Channel and off Land's End. For once the Warleggans had met their match.

He stepped off the mast and, leaning flat on the deck, edged his way towards the poop. The door of the cabin faced him askew. It was an inch or two ajar but jammed. A trickle of water still ran from a corner of it as from the mouth of a sick old man.

He found a spar and thrust it into the door, tried to force it open. The spar splintered but the gap widened. As he got his shoulder into the opening the ship rocked with another great wave. Water flung itself into the air, high, high; as it fell the rest of the wave swirled round the ship, rising to his shoulders; he clung tight, it swirled, dragged, sucked, gave way at last. Water poured from the cabin, deluged him long after the rest had gone. He waited until this too had fallen to his waist before he forced his way in.

Something was tapping gently at his leg. Curious green gloom as if under water.

The three larboard portholes were buried deep, the starboard ones, glass smashed, looked at the sky. A table floating, a periwig, a news sheet. On the upper wall a map still hung. He looked down. The thing tapping his leg was a man's hand. The man floated face downwards, gently, submissively; the water draining out by the door had brought him over to greet Ross. For a second it gave the illusion of life.

Ross caught him by the collar and lifted his head. It was Matthew Sanson.

With a grunt Ross dropped the head back in the water and squeezed his way out into the air.

As the tide went out hundreds waded out and fell on the ship. With axes they burst open the hatches and dragged out the rest of the cargo. A quantity of mixed goods in the rear hatch was undamaged, and more kegs of rum were found. The deck planks were torn up, the wheel and binnacle carried off, the clothing and bits of furniture in the bunks and cabins. Jud, well gone in liquor, was saved from drowning in two feet of water, his arms clasped round the gilt figurehead. He had either mistaken her for a real woman or the gilt for real gold.

As dusk began to fall another bonfire was set up near the ship to light the scavengers on their way. The rising wind blew whorls of smoke flatly across the wet beach where it joined the fires on the sand hills.

Ross left the ship and walked home. He changed his clothes, which were stiff with half-dried salt, had a brief meal and then sat with Demelza. But the restless devil inside himself was not appeased; the pain and the fury were not gone. He went out again in the gathering windy dark.

By the light of a lantern a few of the more sober citizens were burying seven corpses at the foot of the sand hills. Ross stopped to tell them to go deep. He did not want the next spring tide uncovering them. He asked Zacky how many had been saved and was told that two had been taken to Mellin.

He climbed a little and stared down at the crowd round a bonfire. Nick Vigus had brought his flute and people were jigging to his tune. Many were drunk and lay about, too weak to walk home. The wind was bitter, and there would be illness even in this bounty.

A hand caught his arm. It was John Gimlett.

"Beg pardon, sur."

"What is it?"

"The miners, sur. From Illugan an' St. Ann's. The first ones are comin' down the valley. I thought——"

"Are there many?"

"In their 'undreds, Bob Nanfan d'say."

"Well, get you back into the house, man, and bolt the doors. They're only coming to loot the ship."

"Aye, sur, but there's little left to loot — on the ship."

Ross rubbed his chin. "I know. But there's little left to drink either. We shall manage them."

He went down to the beach. He hoped the Illuggan miners had not spent all the daylight hours drinking by the way.

On the beach things were quieter. The bonfire sent a constant shower of sparks chasing across the sand. Just beyond the wreck the surf piled up, a pale mountainous reef in the half-dark.

Then his arm was caught a second time. Pally Rogers from Sawle.

"Look ee! What's that, sur? Isn't it a light?"

Ross stared out to sea.

"Ef that be another ship she's coming ashore too!" said Rogers. "She's too close in to do else. The Lord God ha' mercy on their souls!"

Ross caught the glint of a light beyond the surf. Then he saw a second light close behind. He began to run towards the edge of the sea.

As he neared it the foam came to meet him, detaching itself from the mass and scudding and bowling across the sand in hundreds of flakes of all sizes. He splashed into a few inches of water and stopped, peering, trying to get his breath in the wind. Rogers caught him up.

"Over thur, sur!"

Although the gale had grown again a few stars were out, and you could see well enough. A big ship, bigger than the brigantine, was coming in fast. A light forward and one amidships but no stern light. One minute she seemed right out of the water, and the next only her masts showed. There was no question of manoeuvring to beach her; she was coming in anyhow as the waves threw her about.

Someone aboard had seen how near the end was, for a flare was lit — rags soaked in oil — and it flickered and flared in the wind. Dozens on the beach saw it.

She came in nearer the house than the *Queen Charlotte* and seemed to strike with scarcely a jar. Only her foremast toppling slowly showed the impact.

At the same moment the vanguard of the St. Ann's and Illugan miners streamed on to the beach.

CHAPTER X

Pride of Madras, an East Indiaman homeward bound with a full cargo of silks, tea, and spices, had suddenly appeared, a flying wraith in the fog of the storm, off Sennen in the forenoon of that day.

She had seemed certain to strike Gurnard's Head but the lull in the gale had just given her sea room. Then she had been seen off Godrevy, and a little later the miners of Illuggan and St. Ann's, with news of the *Queen Charlotte* wreck in their ears, had heard that a finer prize was due any minute at Gwithian or Basset's Cove.

So they had pulled two ways, and instead of marching for Nampara had flocked into the gin shops and kiddleys of St. Ann's while scouts kept watch on the cliffs.

She had slipped right under St. Ann's Beacon unseen in the mist, and it was not until just before dusk that she had been picked up again ducking across the mouth of Sawle Cove. She must have come ashore within a few miles, and the miners had followed along the cliffs and down the lanes, so that their leaders reached Hendrawna Beach at the same time as the ship.

What followed would not have been pretty in the sun of a summer afternoon. Happening as it did through a winter's night, starlit in a gale, it was full of the shadowed horror and shrill cadences of another world.

She came in so swiftly that only half a dozen of the locals knew of her until she lit the flare. Then when she struck, everyone began to run towards her. They and the newcomers converged together. Rivalry flared up in a second.

To begin they could not get near her; but the tide had still another two hours to ebb and very soon the venturesome, reckless with rum and gin, plunged through the surf. There was still one light on the ship though the waves were breaking right over her, and two sailors were able to swim ashore, one with a rope. But they could get no one interested enough to hold it, and a third sailor, washed ashore half conscious, was set upon and stripped of his shirt and breeches and left groaning naked on the sand.

Great numbers of miners were now coming, and soon the grey of the sands was black in a huge semicircle before the ship. Ross played no part in it now, either in wreck or rescue. He had edged a little away to watch, but those who saw his face saw no disapproval on it. It was as if the goad of the pain in him would leave him no respite for judgment and sanity.

Others of the crew had got ashore, but now it was the common thing to seize anything they carried, and those who resisted were stripped and roughly handled and left to crawl away as best they could. Two who drew knives were knocked unconscious.

By seven the ship was dry, and by then there were three thousand people on the beach. Barrels in which the pilchards had come ashore were set alight, and these, thick with oil, flared and smoked like giant torches. The ship was a carcase on which a myriad ants crawled. Men were everywhere, hacking with knives and axes, dragging out from the bowels of the ship the riches of the Indies. Dozens lay about the beach, drunk or senseless from a fight. The crew and eight passengers — saved at last by Zacky Martin and Pally Rogers and a few others — broke up into two parties, the larger, led by the mate, going off into the country in search of help, the rest huddling in a group some distance from the ship, while the captain stood guard over them with a drawn sword.

With rich goods seized and fine brandy drunk, fights broke out everywhere. Smouldering feuds between one hamlet and another, one mine and the next, had come to flame. Empty bellies and empty pockets reacted alike to the temptations of the night. To the shipwrecked people it seemed that they had been cast upon the shore of a wild and savage foreign land where thousands of dark-faced men and women talking an uncouth tongue were waiting to tear them to pieces for the clothes they wore.

As the tide began to creep round the ship again Ross went aboard, swarming up by a rope that hung from her bows. He found an orgy of destruction. Men lay drunk about the deck, others fought for a roll of cloth or curtains or cases of tea, often tearing or spilling what they quarrelled over. But the saner men, aware like Ross that time was short, were labouring to clear the ship while she was still intact. Like *Queen Charlotte, Pride of Madras* lay beam on, and another tide might break her up. Lanterns were in the hold, and dozens of men were below passing up goods in a chain to the deck where they were carried to the side and thrown or lowered to others waiting on the sand. These were all St. Ann's men, and farther forward the Illuggan men were doing the same.

Aft he found some from Grambler and Sawle tearing out the panelling in the captain's cabin. Among all the hammering and the shrill squeaks of wood, Paul Daniel slept peacefully in a corner. Ross hauled him to his feet by the collar of his jacket, but Paul only smiled and sank down again.

Jack Cobbledick nodded. "Tes all right, sur. We'll see to 'e when we d'leave."

"Another half-hour is all you can take."

Ross went on deck again. The high wind was pure and cold. He took a deep breath. Above and behind all the shouts, the laughter, the distant singing, the hammering, the scuffles and the groans, was another sound, that of the surf, coming in. It made a noise to-night like hundreds of carts rumbling over wooden bridges.

He avoided two men fighting in the scuppers, went forward and tried to rouse some of the drunks. He spoke of the tide to some of those who were working, had bare nods in exchange.

He stared over the beach. The funnels of fire and smoke from the barrels were still scattering sparks over the sand. Sections of the crowd were lit in umber and orange. Milling faces and black smoke round a dozen funeral pyres. A pagan rite. Back in the sand hills the volcanoes spumed.

He slid over the side, hand by hand down the rope. In water up to his knees.

He pushed his way through the crowd. It seemed as if normal feelings were coming to him. Circulation to a dead limb.

He looked about for the survivors. They were still huddled together just beyond the thickest of the crowd.

As he came near, two of the sailors drew knives and the captain half lifted his sword.

"Keep your distance, man! Keep clear! We'll fight."

Ross eyed them over. A score of shivering exhausted wretches; if they had no attention several might die before morning.

"I was about to offer you shelter," he said.

At the sound of his more cultured voice the captain lowered his sword. "Who are you? What do you want?"

"My name is Poldark. I have a house near here."

There was a whispered consultation. "And you offer us shelter?"

"Such as I have. A fire. Blankets. Something hot to drink."

Even now there was hesitation: they had been so used that they were afraid of treachery. And the captain had some idea of staying here the night to be able to bear his full witness to the courts. But the eight passengers overruled him.

"Very well, sir," said the captain, keeping his sword unsheathed, "if you will lead the way."

Ross inclined his head and moved off slowly across the beach. The captain fell into step beside him, the two armed sailors followed close behind and the rest straggled after.

They passed several dozen people dancing round a fire and drinking fresh-brewed tea (ex *Pride of Madras*) laced with brandy (ex *Pride of Madras*). They overtook six mules laden so heavy with rolls of cloth that their feet sank inches in the sand at every step. They skirted forty or fifty men fighting in a pack for four gold ingots.

The captain said in a voice trembling with indignation:

"Have you any control over these — these savages?"

"None whatever," Ross said.

"Is there no law in this land?"

"None which will stand before a thousand miners."

"It — it is a disgrace. A crying disgrace. Two years ago I was shipwrecked off Patagonia — and treated less barbarously."

"Perhaps the natives were better fed than we in this district."

"Fed? Food — oh, if it were food we carried and these men were starving——"

"Many have been near it for months."

"— then there might be some excuse. But it is not food. To pillage the ship, and we ourselves barely escaped with our lives! I never thought such a day could be! It is monstrous!"

"There is much in this world which is monstrous," Ross said. "Let us be thankful they were content with your shirts."

The captain glanced at him. A passing

lantern showed up the taut, lean, overstrained face, the pale scar, the half-lidded eyes. The captain said no more.

As they climbed the wall at the end of the beach they saw a group of men coming towards them from Nampara House. Ross stopped and stared. Then he caught the creak of leather.

"Here is the law you were invoking."

The men came up. A dozen dismounted troopers in the charge of a sergeant. Captain McNeil and his men had been moved some months before, and these were strangers. They had marched out from Truro on hearing of the wreck of the *Queen Charlotte*.

This much the sergeant was explaining when the captain burst in with an angry flood of complaint, and soon he was surrounded by the passengers and crew, demanding summary justice. The sergeant plucked at his lip and stared across at the beach, which stirred and quickened with a wild and sinister life of its own.

"You go down there at your own risk, Sergeant," Ross said.

There was a sudden silence, followed by another babel of threat and complaint from the shipwrecked people.

"All right," said the sergeant. "Go easy. Go easy now, we'll put a stop to the looting, never you fear. We'll see no more is carried away. We'll put a stop to it."

"You would be advised to delay until daylight," Ross said. "The night will have cooled tempers. Remember the two customs officers who were killed at Gwithian last year."

"I have me orders, sir." The sergeant glanced uneasily at his small band and then again at the struggling smoky mass on the beach. "We'll see all this is put a stop to." He patted his musket.

"I warn you," Ross said, "half of them are in drink and many fighting among themselves. If you interfere they'll stop their quarrelling and turn on you. And so far it has been fists and a few sticks. But if you fire into them not half of you will come out of it alive."

The sergeant hesitated again. "Ye'd advise me to wait until first light?"

"It is your only hope."

The captain burst out again, but some of the passengers, shivering and half dead from exposure, cut him short and pleaded to be led to shelter.

Ross went on to the house, leaving the troopers still hesitant on the edge of the maelstrom. At the door of the house he stopped again.

"You'll pardon me, gentlemen, but may I ask you for quietness. My wife is just recovering from a grave illness and I do not wish to disturb her."

The chattering and muttering slowly died away to silence.

He led the way in.

CHAPTER XI

Ross woke at the first light. He had slept heavily for seven hours. The inescapable pain was still there but some emotional purging of the night had deadened its old power. It was the first time for a week he had undressed, the first full sleep he had had. He had gone up to his old room, for Demelza had seemed better last night, and Jane Gimlett said she would sleep in the chair before the fire.

He dressed quickly, stiffly, but was quiet about it. Below him in the parlour and in the next two rooms twenty-two men were sleeping. Let them lie. All the strain of last night had brought the stiffness of the French musket wound back, and it was with a sharp limp that he went to the window. The wind was still high and the glass thick with salt. He opened the window and stared out on Hendrawna Beach.

Dawn had just broken, and in a clear sky seven black clouds were following each other across the lightening east like seven ill-begotten sons of the storm. The tide was nearly out and both wrecks were dry. The *Queen Charlotte*, lying almost deserted, might have been an old whale cast up by the sea. Around and about the *Pride of Madras* people still milled and crawled. The sands were patchy with people, and at first he thought Leisure Cliff and those east of it had been decorated by some whim of the revellers. Then he saw that the wind had been the only reveller, and costly silks had been blown from the wreck and hung in inaccessible places all along the beach and cliffs. Goods and stores were still scattered on the sand hills and just above high-water mark, but a large part was already gone.

There had been bloodshed in the night.

Jack Cobbledick, calling in just before midnight, had told him that the troopers had gone down to the beach and tried to stand guard over the wreck. But the tide had driven them off and the wreckers had gone on with salvaging their prizes as if the solders had not existed. The sergeant, trying to get his way by peaceful measures, was roughly handled; and some of the soldiers fired into the air to scare the crowd. Then they had been forced off the beach step by step with a thousand angry men following them.

A little later an Illuggan miner had been caught molesting a St. Ann's woman, and a huge fight had developed which had only been broken by the inrush of the sea threatening to carry off the booty, and not before a hundred or more men were stretched out on the beach.

Ross did not know whether the troopers had again tried to take over the wreck when the tide went back, but he thought not. It was more likely that they still kept discreet watch in the sand hills while the sergeant sent for reinforcements.

But in another six hours the ships would be nothing but hulks, every plank and stick carried away, the bones picked clean.

He closed the window, and as the rimed glass shut out the view the pang of his own personal loss returned. He had planned so much for Julia, had watched her grow from a scarcely separable entity, seen her nature unfold, the very beginning of traits and characteristics make their quaint showing. It was hardly believable that now they would never develop, that all that potential sweetness should dry up at its fount and turn to dust. Hardly believable and hardly bearable.

He slowly put on his coat and waistcoat and limped downstairs.

In the bedroom Jane Gimlett slept soundly before a fire that had gone out. Demelza was awake.

He sat beside the bed and she slipped her hand into his. It was thin and weak, but there was a returning firmness underneath.

"How are you?"

"Much, much better. I slept all the night through. Oh, Ross. Oh, my dear, I can feel the strength returning to me. In a few days more I shall be up."

"Not yet awhile."

"And did you sleep?"

"Like the——" He changed his smile. "Like one drugged."

She squeezed his hand. "An' all the folk from the ship?"

"I have not been to see."

She said: "I have never seen a real shipwreck, not in daytime. Not a proper one."

"Soon I'll carry you up to our old bedroom and you can see it all through the spyglass."

"This morning?"

"Not this morning."

"I wish it was not this time o' year," she said. "I seem to be tired for the summer."

"It will come."

There was a pause.

"I believe to-morrow will be too late to see the best of the wreck."

"Hush, or you'll wake Jane."

"Well, you could wrap me in blankets an' I should come to no harm."

He sighed and put her hand against his cheek. It was not a disconsolate sigh, for her returning life was a tonic to his soul.

Whatever she suffered, whatever loss came to her, she would throw it off, for it was not in her nature to go under. Although she was the woman and he a fierce and sometimes arrogant man, hers was the stronger nature because the more pliant. That did not mean that she did not feel Julia's death as deeply and as bitterly, but he saw that she would recover first. It might be because he had had all the other failures and disappointments. But chiefly it was because some element had put it in her nature to be happy. She was born so and could not change. He thanked God for it. Wherever she went and however long she lived she would be the same, lavishing interest on the things she loved and contriving for their betterment, working for and bringing up her children. . . .

Ah, there was the rub.

He found she was looking at him.

"Have you heard of them at Trenwith?" she asked.

"Not since I told you before." He looked at her and saw that despite her loss there was no trace of bitterness in her thoughts of Elizabeth and Francis. It made him ashamed of his own.

"Did they say there was any loss among those who were in the *Pride of Madras?*"

"None of the passengers. Some of the crew."

She sighed. "Ross, I b'lieve the miners, the Illuggan and St. Ann's miners, have made a rare mess of the garden. I heard 'em trampling over it all last evening, and Jane said they had mules and donkeys with them."

"If anything is damaged it can be put to right," Ross said.

"Was Father amongst them, did you see?"

"I saw nothing of him."

"Maybe he is reformed in that way too. Though I doubt there must have been many Methodies among those who came. I wonder what — what he will say about this. . . ."

Ross knew she was not referring to the wreck.

"Nothing that can make any difference, my dear. Nothing could have made any difference."

"She nodded. "I know. Sometimes I wonder if she ever really stood any chance.""

"Why?"

"I don't know, Ross. She seemed to have it so bad from the start. And she was so young. . . .""

There was a long silence.

At length Ross got up and pulled the curtain back. Even this did not wake Jane Gimlett. The sun had risen and was gilding the waving treetops in the valley.

As he came back to the bed Demelza wiped her eyes.

"I think, I believe I like you with a beard, Ross."

He put his hand up. "Well, I do not like myself. It will come off sometime to-day."

"Is it going to be a fine day, do you think?"

"Fine enough."

"I wish I could see the sun. That is the drawback to this room, there is no sun until afternoon."

"Well, so soon as you are well you shall go upstairs again."

"Ross, I should like to see our room again. Take me up, just for a few minutes, please. I believe I could walk up if I tried."

On an emotional impulse he said: "Very well; if you wish it."

He lifted her out of the bed, wrapped a blanket round her legs, two round her shoulders, picked her up. She had lost a lot of weight, but somehow the feel of her arm about his neck, the living companionable substance of her, was like a balm. Still quiet to avoid rousing Jane, he slipped out of the room, mounted the creaking stair. He carried her into their bedroom, set her down on the bed. Then he went to the window and opened one to clean a circle in the salt of the other. He shut the window and went back to the bed. Tears were streaming down her face.

"What is wrong?"

"The cot," she said. "I had forgotten the cot."

He put his arm about her and they sat quiet for a minute or two. Then he picked her up again and took her to the window and sat her in a chair.

She stared out on the scene, and with his cheek pressed against hers he stared with her. She took up a corner of the blanket and tried to stop the tears.

She said: "How pretty the cliffs look with all those streamers on 'em."

"Yes."

"Redruth Fair," she said. "The beach puts me in mind of that, the day after it is over."

"It will take some clearing, but the sea is a good scavenger."

"Ross," she said, "I should like you to make it up with Francis sometime. It would be better all round."

"Sometime."

"Sometime soon."

"Sometime soon." He had no heart to argue with her to-day.

The sun shone full upon her face, showing the thin cheeks and the pallid skin.

"When something happens," she said, "like what has just happened to us, it makes all our quarrels seem small and mean, as if we were quarrelling when we hadn't the right. Didn't we ought to find all the friendship we can?"

"If friendship is to be found."

"Yes. But didn't we ought to seek it? Can't all our quarrels be buried and forgot, so that Verity can come to visit us and we go to Trenwith and we can — can live in friendship and not hatred while there's time."

Ross was silent. "I believe yours is the only wisdom, Demelza," he said at length.

They watched the scene on the beach.

"I shan't have to finish that frock for Julia now," she said. "It was that dainty too."

"Come," he said. "You will be catching cold."

"No. I am quite warm, Ross. Let me stay a little longer in the sun."